PENGUIN BOOKS

LOCAL HERO

David Benedictus is a well-known author, director and broadcaster. He has written many novels including *The Fourth of June*, which he adapted for the stage at the St Martin's Theatre, *The Rabbi's Wife* and *A Twentieth Century Man*. He has written and directed for television and the stage where his work includes a number of musicals. He has broadcast on several popular radio programmes including 'Any Questions', 'Woman's Hour', 'A Word in Edgeways' and 'Kaleidoscope'. He has also written two books on collecting antiques and was antiques correspondent for the *Evening Standard*. He lives in Twickenham.

A brilliant film director and scriptwriter, Bill Forsyth's previous films are *That Sinking Feeling* and the enormously successful *Gregory's Girl* for which he won the British Academy Award for the best script.

David Benedictus

LOCAL HERO

Based on a Screenplay by
Bill Forsyth

Penguin Books

Penguin Books Ltd, Harmondsworth,
Middlesex, England
Penguin Books, 40 West 23rd Street,
New York, New York 10010, U.S.A.
Penguin Books Australia Ltd, Ringwood,
Victoria, Australia
Penguin Books Canada Limited, 2801 John Street,
Markham, Ontario, Canada L3R 1B4
Penguin Books (N.Z.) Ltd, 182–190 Wairau Road,
Auckland 10, New Zealand

First published 1983

Printed in the United States of America by
Offset Paperback Mfrs., Inc., Dallas, Pennsylvania
Set in Photina

What is this life, if full of care
We have no time to stand and stare?

W. H. DAVIES

I

HOUSTON

It's not like Mexico, Macintyre

Happer did not make mistakes. Unless it is a mistake to be born in Houston, heir to Knox Oil and Gas, and to add to that massive financial empire acquisitions on a scale that impressed even Texans . . . Happer did not regard it as a mistake, for he often boasted about his great good luck in inheriting one fortune and his cleverness in making several more. If Happer had a vice it was conceit, and if he ever made a mistake it was in hiring Moritz, the celebrated Houston analyst. Later he was to admit, even to himself, that that had been, beyond doubt, a mistake. Perhaps his conceit had led him to hire Moritz; Moritz deduced as much. It was throwing down a challenge to the therapist; find something wrong with me! And since Moritz's vice was also his conceit, he felt sure that he could find plenty wrong with Happer. The more he could find, the longer the treatment would last. The longer it lasted, the more Moritz would rake in. The more Moritz raked in, the more Happer would admire him. The more Happer admired Moritz, the easier it would be for Moritz to find things wrong with Happer.

'You're a piece of crap, Happer, floating in a sea of garbage.'

Happer took this sitting down, his expression bland and considerate.

'All I see, Happer, is failure. I look for signs of a complete human being, but failure's all I see. How much do you make in a week, Happer? Five million dollars?'

'Gross,' says Happer. Now Moritz is speaking his language, Moritz, as a tax deduction, ought to understand these things.

'OK. Gross, and you're still a flop. You make me want to laugh.' Moritz never laughed, except when terrified, when he laughed like a monkey. 'No, you make me want to cry, that's what you make me want to do.' Moritz never cried. An analyst should not seem fallible like ordinary mortals. Moritz once saw a Rabbi cry; in analysis. Moritz was shocked to the core. Fallibility is for the paying customers, but not when the paying customer is a fellow professional.

'Even with two billion dollars you can't make a right move – what have you achieved with all that money and the power that goes with it, eh? Let *me* tell *you*. There's the Happer Tower and Happer Boulevard and Happer College at the University and the Happer Science Foundation – that name sure keeps cropping up, don't it just? – and let us not forget the Happer Observatory, no Sir – a fifty million dollar toy for a sad flop of a man.'

Moritz's attack had the effect of deepening Happer's gloom. He had not been convinced by the man's arguments, but felt bound to listen to the highest paid analyst in Texas. However, some things were sacred, and this attack on the observatories could not pass unchallenged.

'Astronomy is a key science,' Happer announced. This he believed. The sky was so much vaster than the earth that it could not be ignored; and if so paltry a lump of rock as the moon could affect the tides, then what about Venus and Saturn, what about the myriads of constellations still to be discovered? But Moritz scoffed.

'You're on a huge ego trip, man, and you want to drag the whole universe in on it. Tell me about your Comet Project, Happer, go on, I need a good laugh.'

Happer knew that Moritz wouldn't laugh when he told him, but told him all the same. He had spoken to no one about this project since he installed the equipment, and now he was telling Moritz, whom he despised. The analyst certainly knew how to get people to talk.

'It's just a surveillance project . . . looking for a new comet is all.'

'And what are you going to call this comet if and when you find it, Happer?'

Happer knew what Moritz was after, but could not suppress his pleasure as he announced: 'The Happer Comet or Happer's Comet or Comet Happer.' It would be in the text books. His name would survive, not through his sons – for he had no children – but through a comet! Let other men travel five continents to net a butterfly or struggle for half a century to produce a new variety of rose, he would have a *comet*. Of course it should bear his name: should it be Comet Moritz? Moritz pranced around, head weaving like a boxer's, halitosis filtering through his absurd moustache.

'I thought it might be! The whole world will weep with gratitude, Happer, when the big day comes! Mr Happer's got a comet – hurray! But what an empty – when you come right down to it – hollow – I mean, really, Happer – wasteful activity.' Now Moritz's voice took on the concerned regret of the surrogate father. It was the tone in which God spoke to Jonah, or Jesus to Simon Peter, or Paul to the Galatians. 'You're chasing comets around the sky, but is your own life on this earth so complete? What about a wife, children, a family? Are these human goals too simple for you? Oh, Happer!'

But Happer had had enough. Something within him suggested that he need not prolong this, that he only had to press the buzzer on his desk and Moritz would be removed, the pain would cease. 'Out!' he cried, 'Out, out, out, that's enough for today. So out!'

It worked. Like a pricked balloon Moritz shrivelled before his eyes, and his voice became a sycophantic whine!

'Yes, Sir, Mr Happer. It seemed to go well today, didn't it, Sir?'

'It was OK, Moritz.'

'Maybe we could build up the sessions to two or three a week . . . we've reached a crucial stage, Sir.'

'See Mrs Wyatt on the way out.' And Moritz's ingratiating head vanished behind the massive door of Happer's office, a door cut from a single Californian Redwood, and electronically operated. Happer was suddenly terrified and called him back. Two scared men in a vast office.

'Moritz – Moritz, did you mean any of that stuff about me being a flop?'

'God, *no*, Mr Happer, Sir, it's merely basic therapy technique. You can get all that from a video programme. Maybe I got a bit carried away . . .'

'Maybe if I had married,' said Happer, as images of possible wives flicked through his mind like the pages of a Model Directory – but he could see none of these glossy creatures cooking an omelette, 'things would have been different.'

But Moritz had not been hired to deal with a married Happer, nor had he any solutions to the problems of a happy marriage. Indeed, to a therapist happiness is as much of an affront as a miracle is to an atheist. Moritz had to improvise.

'By no means, Mr Happer. The modern world offers many alternatives to the security of the family unit.' Improvisation – never a success. The mention of security made Moritz wince, as Happer's face took on the expression of a child deprived of a treat.

'Look at me, Mr Happer,' Moritz added in desperation, 'I'm a single man.' Happer looked at him and despised what he saw. 'Out! Get out! And stay out!' And this time Moritz went, and the Californian Redwood remained secure against his return.

Humiliation therapy over for another humiliating week, Happer felt hungry. His private apartment was a penthouse suite adjoining his office on the top floor of Knox Oil and Gas, and it was there that he cooked himself his nightly omelette. He had bred the chickens, fed them on a by-product of Knox Oil, set them against tax, and it was appropriate that he should eat the eggs. As he broke one, expertly, with a single hand into a basin, he noticed a tiny red speck. Life beginning within the shell of an egg, and within the eggshell of the sky a dark hole – or a million of them – life ending. All around him the universe was on the move, but within him it was frozen. Did Moritz guess? Happer knew. He whisked the egg fiercely like a man who fears the worst. When he had eaten it he would return to his office, transform it at the press of a button to a massive observatory, and peer through the radio telescope at ... Happer's Comet? Would it be tonight? If only astronomers could chart space as thoroughly as meteorologists did the atmosphere, but they were a lazy bunch. He, Happer, knew what it meant to be up all night peering at immensities of emptiness. *They* would rather glance at the moon, then go to bed, where their silly wives would be waiting. Scientists? Mere dabblers. The omelette was excellent. Happer was himself again.

Macintyre too was spending a solitary evening. He had been ploughing through *Playboy* philosophy over a TV dinner, and he was impressed, as always, at the wisdom of a mere magazine with naked girls in it. How did they know all that stuff? And how come with magazines that knew so much, America seemed always to get landed with Presidents who knew so little? It was crazy. What was crazy too was that Macintyre, who was in every way that mattered the archetype of a *Playboy* playboy, was spending another solitary evening, maybe even his last evening in Houston for some time. *Playboy* had suggested he buy a Turbo Porsche with a Sanyo Quadrophenic system; he had done so. *Playboy* had had him install his colour video equipment with extra-speedy search facilities; he had done so. *Playboy* had recommended his Gene Autrey outfit, which, when he caught a glimpse of himself in the full-length smoky mirror in the Louis Quinze frame, looked, he thought, extremely silly; and from advertisements in *Playboy* he had selected a wide range of cosmetics, a pure silk kimono embroidered with passages from *I Ching*, and – greatly daring – black condoms in the special giant packet. He had made use of every page in the magazine, but the use to which he had put the pages of naked girls was self-defeating – and the special offer giant packet remained sealed. Well, there were not likely to be girls as readily available in Scotland as in Houston – did they even have *Playboy* in Scotland? – *Christ!* – and he really felt he owed himself a good time. This night of all nights.

Having disposed of the TV dinner in the garbage disposal he decided to ring Angela, but Angela's answering service had a supercilious tone so he rang Trudi. Heidi, whom he always regarded as a thoroughly bad influence on Trudi, answered the phone, and pretended not to recognize his voice.

'For Christ's sake, Heidi, it's Mac – yeah, M – A – C, Trudi knows, yeah, just get her, willya?'

While waiting Mac reflected that in *Playboy* fiction room-mates of girl-friends are usually easy lays, but laying Heidi would be about as much fun as laying a carpet. Did Heidi screw? Hey, maybe she screwed Trudi . . .

'Hello there, Trudi, how are you? Good. I'm terrific too. Now listen, baby, it's just that I have to leave town for a while – Scotland, would you believe – there are still some things of yours parked here in my apartment ... *what* things? ... well, there's some mail, and three letters, yeah, they've been here a while I'm afraid ... what else is there ... your cigarette lighter, the English one ... just thought, Trudi, that you might be missing that, no it's not *important*, baby, not if you can live without it ... no listen, Trudi, there is something else. You remember my camera case, the Nikon, the one you kept your make-up in, I want it back ... No, that's not why I phoned, lover, I only thought ... Trudi, I am *not* calling you a thief, no, I don't want to argue about it ... yeah, well all right you are a thief, aren't you, a god-damn kleptomaniac ... yeah, maybe you *should* see a doctor, because you're so right, it is a perversion, you bet your sweet ass ... oh go piss up a rope!'

The effect of this call was so disastrous that Mac had to take giant strides up and down his deep-pile reproduction Azerbaijan carpet to calm his anger and desolation. As he did so, he called Trudi all the names he had wanted to call her on the telephone. He should have done. He was never likely to see her again now. The only thing for it was to call Lester about the Porsche. Good old Lester, a mechanical genius; he could not leave the car in better hands. He told Lester that when Lester answered. It was not necessary to flatter the man because he paid him a healthy sum to keep the car in order, but surely to God there was nothing wrong in showing Lester how much he admired him – that was another thing *Playboy* had always insisted upon: you should show your feelings rather than bottle them up. And respect artisans. He told Lester that he wanted the suspension fixed and the fuel injection; also the 145 plugs ought to be replaced and the differential checked – 'I'm losing some tread on the nearside' – but Lester understood all that. Mac promised to leave a list in the car and the keys with Stoller downstairs if Lester would come and pick the machine up on, maybe, Thursday. Lester said he would.

'Oh and man, you don't have to test-drive it all the way to

New Orleans and back, you dig?' (Why did Mac always use out-of-date hip-talk to Lester just because the car was black? I mean, like crass, man.)

Lester promised to go no further than Kansas City, and rang off. *Kansas City?*

Happer had stayed up all night staring into space. There had been no new comet. There had been lots of activity out there with the usual old planets and a Qasar he was taking a paternal interest in and a star-cluster that showed signs of regrouping as well as the junk-yard that the space scientists were for ever hurling up there like children skimming stones into the sea — there was, in short, as much traffic in space as in Downtown Houston, and he, Happer, was a traffic-cop of space. But no new comet. The problem was partly Houston; a pig of a place to observe from, with its congested air-waves and neon fool-ishness. He must get out to one of the big observatories, but that meant leaving Happer Tower which he had not done now for, *Jeesus*, could it be five years? If he could only get to Australia, or Africa, or . . . Scotland? But wasn't young Macintyre going to Scotland on the Ferness Project? He called Mrs Wyatt, and she confirmed that Fountain of Acquisitions had indeed chosen Macintyre, who had had such a success with the Mexico busi-ness, and who, of course, was part-Scottish.

'Have him up here to see me, Mrs Wyatt.'

'You have the Executive Board Meeting at ten, Mr Happer.' Happer had forgotten. To forget the Executive — a sign that he was cracking up. Testily he snapped:

'Well have him see me after the Board.'

'But His Serene Highness is scheduled for midday —'

'Then His Serene Highness will just have to wait. He comes from an ancient culture; right then, he's used to waiting.'

The first item on the Board's agenda was to view and approve a documentary about the involvement of Knox Oil and Gas in

North Sea Oil exploration. A documentary is a film without any girls in it. The documentary was exceptionally dull. To view it, the blinds had been drawn in the boardroom and the lights turned out. Happer, as we already know, had been up all night. As Happer snored, the voice of the commentator, a full octave lower than the voice of ordinary mortals – did they feed them anabolic steroids? – droned on:

'Nature guards her treasures jealously. Just a decade ago these oil fields were beyond our reach. We did not have the technology. Today a Knox engineer may tell you over a friendly beer that he might need a little longer but he'll get the oil, for he knows that a little time is all that we have left . . .'

The pictures did not show the Knox engineer enjoying a friendly beer, but they did show massive rigs and floating platforms and heaving waves, and the music which accompanied them suggested great battles against the might of Pharaoh, and chariot races, and the triumph, after many trials and much tribulation, of Good over Evil. At the culminating moment of this elemental battle, the Knox Oil logo was fixed on the screen in majestic isolation, and the music crashed to silence and the lights came up in the boardroom, and all that could be heard was the unmajestic sound of Happer snoring.

Had it not been that Happer owned the boardroom, and the building of which it was a part, and the film which he had just snored through, and the dozen or so attentive people in the boardroom with Happer, he might have thought it tactless to continue snoring. As things were, however, he just went right on, despite the activity of the technicians who removed from the boardroom the projector and the screen. And here was a dilemma for the Board of Knox Oil and Gas. Who could reserve to themselves the right to nudge Happer awake in full view of his colleagues? It needed a Great Man (like Alexander Haig) to take control in a crisis, and none was present. The situation was exacerbated when the coffee cup, which had been crooked

over Happer's little finger, thudded to the floor, and the thick
black slick of sugared coffee crept across the nylon pile.

Had it not been for Mrs Wyatt entering the room, they might
have been sitting there still. Mrs Wyatt, as the second most
important person in Knox Oil and Gas, gave Happer a vigorous
shake. The rest of the Board watched, much as the chorus
watches in Greek tragedy when the messenger arrives to tell
the King in iambic pentameters the news that battles have been
lost, queens and princesses raped, and the weather particularly
bad for the time of year.

But Happer woke fast and, smiling at Mrs Wyatt, apologized
to those around him in a pleasant manner. When a young aide
rashly commented that he found the human dimension at the
end of the documentary very, well, *human*, and, as an angle, a
particularly good, well, *angle*, Happer stared at him in bewilder-
ment. What movie? There was no trace of a movie. The man
was talking in absolute riddles. (He had also forfeited his future
as an executive with Knox Oil and Gas.)

It was Crabbe who, with a glance at the young aide in which
pity was mingled with contempt – there, but for the grace of
God, thought Crabbe, went Crabbe, took control of the meeting,
to expand the great news that, while North Sea Oil had been a
good girl, she had outlived her usefulness and that the time had
come to take up with a new and more glamorous girl, known
as North Atlantic Oil. He moved over to a wall-chart as he said:

'The main business therefore, Mr Happer, gentlemen, is to
report on the progress of our acquisition of Scotland – well, *part*
of Scotland, for our refinery and storage space. As you know we
have a two-year lead in the North Atlantic, and this could be
doubled if we could find an appropriate site for a terminal and
streamline the processing end of things offshore. With a de-
ductible ten-year loan of two hundred million from Knox
Financial against a total investment of six hundred million, and
with Knox Real Estate handling the holding on the site and the

construction, the whole deal will be kept one hundred per cent in the family.'

Fountain of Acquisitions then explained that his survey teams had found the only suitable bay on the entire North-Atlantic coastline, with a natural bedrock harbour and a near-by sedimentary bay, which would be – *will* be – perfect for piling in the pumping installations.

Crabbe resumed to point out that the British Government, pressed by the Highlands and Islands Development Board, was prepared to build a new highway from Glasgow, which road would be financed by a thirty-year loan from Knox European, the loan being based on a fixed exchange rate, which Knox Advisory reckoned was historically unrealistic, so that as Crabbe vividly put it: 'We've got 'em by the nuts!'

Fountain answered the unspoken question which had been hovering on the pinched lips of Kleber of Accounts by revealing that the sum set aside over a three-year period for the acquisition of Ferness Bay was . . . sixty million dollars.

Crabbe leapt in to emphasize the importance of getting a negotiator on the site at once. 'We're dealing, gentlemen, with close and stable allies of the US, not to mention the close historic links between Knox Oil and Scotland. This is not a third world situation: it is a matter of public relations, and a highly skilled man-to-man confrontation. We need the human dimension to swing this one.'

'Macintyre,' said Happer.

'Exactly, Sir,' said Fountain.

'He's young,' Crabbe warned.

'He's hungry,' said Fountain.

'I'm seeing him,' said Happer. '*Now*,' said Happer. 'Mrs Wyatt,' said Happer, and rose from his chair.

'Gentlemen . . .' said Mrs Wyatt, and they all dispersed, the young aide never to be seen again in the boardroom of Knox Oil and Gas.

*

Fountain had primed Macintyre thoroughly about the Scotland trip. Macintyre had wanted to know why he couldn't do the whole thing by Telex, as he had Mexico – 'I'm a Telex man' – but Fountain explained that he would be dealing with people like himself, not just another bunch of Indians. Public relations would be involved; diplomacy would be what would swing it, and, if it swings, Mac had Fountain's word that promotion would follow as surely as Roebuck followed Sears.

But there had still been something troubling the lad, and he had not wanted to mention it to Fountain. So when he got the summons from Happer's office, he had taken Calvin Wrain of Negotiations along the corridor to the hot-food dispenser, which a technical friend had told him could not be bugged because of the temperature variations, and bought them both the Chilli dinner. As he fed the American presidents into the Chilli dinner slot he asked Calvin whether he would look after Africa in his absence.

'We've got the Congo Development Minister's tit in the wringer, and he's ready to cough up another five per cent of the gross. Give him a five days' deadline. A coupla telexes will take care of it, Cal. And Cal – I've a confession to make. Fountain thinks I'm a Scotchman and Happer – apparently – thinks I'm a Scotchman –'

'And you're not a Scotchman? How come, Mac?'

'My folks changed their name when they got off the boat from Hungary. They thought Macintyre was American. They didn't know from nothing, Cal. My real name's a bitch of a name. It hasn't got enough vowels in it, and the ones it has got are the *wrong* ones. Shit, Cal, would they send me to Scotland if they knew?'

'Hell, they gave you Mexico, and Macintyre sure isn't a Mexican name.'

'Yeah, but that was a telex job, and everyone knows I can handle telex work.' At this point Mac's attempts to wrest the top off his pot of chilli resulted in a smudge of scalding fluid on his tie. As Cal wiped him down with a handkerchief, he expatiated on the origins of his own name Calvin Wrain III.

'My folks were Red Indian way back – Rainwater, but they dropped the "water" and stuck a "W" on the front and now we're whiter than white. Don't worry, Mac. Ask yourself what kind of a name Happer is when you get right down to it.'

But Mac had worried and did worry and the worry was only slightly alleviated by getting to ride in the express elevator that was for the exclusive use of Happer himself and the selected few fortunate enough to be summoned into his presence. Mac was enjoying his ride which was smoother than any Porsche and was wondering whether it was the Ivy League thing to tip the elevator hop when the elevator hop put him down – don't they always? – with: 'There's chilli sauce on your tie, sir.' With Mac's first sight of the Happer penthouse, he realized that *Playboy* had got it all wrong; There was more to life than musical decanters and expensive video equipment. An antique telescope made by Sir Isaac Newton stood on its tripod, its engraved brass blazing with reflected light. Globes and orreries hung suspended on invisible wires. Dutch navigational charts covered the walls and vast photographs of the surfaces of the moon, Mars and Venus made it seem as though each step on the thick charcoal-coloured carpet was a giant step for mankind. Halfway to Happer's kingdom sat Mrs Wyatt, the second most important person in Houston and in Texas, and therefore, arguably, the third most important person in the US of A.

'Take a seat Mr Macintyre,' she said, and Mac was relieved to find a seat beneath him. He sat and listened to Mrs Wyatt at work – she pressed a button on the Intercom. It was like a dream.

'Yes? I'm sorry Your Excellency, but Mr Happer is in a meeting right now. Perhaps you could tell His Holiness that Mr Happer will be free in half an hour. No, I am very much afraid that I am not at liberty to give you Mr Happer's private number – alas, no. Thank you for calling, Sir.'

Mrs Wyatt pressed another button.

'I have the Prime Minister for you now, Mr Happer . . . hold on . . . Mr Happer, ma'am . . . yes, I did, ma'am, I tried it with raspberries. It was quite delicious, although I could only get the frozen – yes, ma'am, here's Mr Happer now, have a nice day.'

As she put down the telephone, Mac was suddenly concerned about the condition of his tie and asked Mrs Wyatt if he could use the washroom, and she directed him towards it, but he had only dampened the tie when her voice, quadrophonically amplified, commanded him to *please* join Mr Happer, who was waiting for him. Mac did not need to be told twice (or, quadrophonically, eight times).

His first sight of Happer, however, was reassuring. The man was big but not mountainous. Distinguished-looking but not godlike. Well dressed, but not in ermine. He appeared to have nicked himself shaving just to the left of the small grey moustache. But the desk he sat behind was truly formidable. No more impressive slabs of wood could have been seen since King Arthur.

'Macintyre, Sir. Pleased to meet you.'

Happer's voice was paternal, but stern.

'You're going to Scotland, Macintyre.'

Now why, thought Macintyre, does a man like that have a desk like that? A man, thought Macintyre, should be *more* impressive than the desk behind which he sits. And why, thought Happer, does a young man like that wear a tie like that? To be so ambitious, to work so hard, to be honoured with such an interview leading to such an opportunity, and then to wear a tie resembling beef stew, was very odd.

'Yes, Sir,' Macintyre said, and his fingers, being aware of the direction of Happer's glance, went halfway to his tie and then returned to his thighs as though the thing was beyond redemption, which it was.

'It's like going home, like *we're* going home, eh Macintyre?'
Happer's face wrenched itself into a kind of investment adviser's
smile, as he continued: 'The founder of all this was a Scot –
Alexander Knox from the town of Nairn.'

Happer nodded an acknowledgement at the portrait that
appeared to be a stern Victorian paterfamilias (oil on canvas,
indistinctly signed and dated, carved wooden frame), who could
have been a baptist preacher or a millionaire or both, such
things not being unknown in Scotland. Mac smiled as suitable
a smile as he could muster at the portrait, until Happer told
him: 'That's not Knox, that's my father, who bought him out in
1912. It would have been handy if he had thought to change
the name of the company at the same time, but . . . anyway
you're going to Scotland, eh Macintyre, the auld countree?'

Happer's attempt at an appropriate accent was accompanied
by him screwing his face up into what he fancied might be an
auld Scottish face. Macintyre agreed. There was little else to do.
Almost casually Happer continued:

'Virgo is well up this time of year . . .' and then leaned back
in his chair to assess the impact of the remark. But all Mac
could manage was a sophomoric: 'Sir?'

'I'm talking about the sky, Macintyre. The constellation of
Virgo is very prominent in the sky just now in Scotland.' Happer
paused to allow Macintyre to interject something creative but
again the young man failed him. Did Fountain of Acquisitions
really know what he was doing? This was a major undertaking. 'I want you to keep an eye on Virgo for me. Will you do
that?'

Macintyre remained confused. He knew he was not doing
himself justice, and wished to say so, but if he did he might be
drawing attention to what Happer, who seemed to be something
of an eccentric, might just have failed to notice. Meanwhile
Happer had pressed a couple of switches concealed within a
drawer in the remarkable desk, and the ceiling parted in the

middle like a huge eye opening while the automatic blinds covered the windows. Suddenly it was dusk. Stars could be seen twinkling in the deep purple of the night sky. Mac shivered. Happer took him by the arm and led him to the centre of the room. Mac's eyes were wide, the pupils dilated. Happer pointed up:

'This,' he said with paternal pride, 'is Virgo. Find the Great Bear, the Big Dipper, and you can't go wrong. Get to recognize Virgo. I'm expecting something special from there, Macintyre. Keep your eyes skinned. I shall want reports.'

'Reports, Sir?'

'Reports, of course, *reports*. Anything unusual in Virgo. It might look like a new star, or even a shooting star. Whatever it is, I want to know about it. Reports. Anything out of the ordinary, you phone me, night or day. This' – and he handed him an embossed card – 'is my private number. Only three people in the world have this number, Macintyre, and one of them is dead.'

'Does that three include yourself, Sir?' Macintyre asked, impressed and keen to get a clear view of the situation. But Happer was not a man to get hung up over details.

'You are travelling six hours east of here, so you'll be ahead of me. Think of that!'

Macintyre thought about it in terms of telexes. Then he understood.

'You know what I'm talking about?' Happer insisted. In the gloom of the artificial night his face had a bluish tinge to it, like (Macintyre supposed) one newly risen from the dead. Macintyre longed to be in his Porsche with Trudi by his side listening to Carole King. He had no wish to go to Scotland and look at stars. But there was still a question hanging in the air, and he had to give some sort of an answer.

'I have a general, um,' he said, but Happer seemed scarcely to listen.

'You'll know it when you see it. And you'll telephone me,

OK?' Happer returned to his chair. A great man. Macintyre said nothing. Suddenly Happer seemed apprehensive.

'You know what a comet is, don't you?'

'I feel sure that I'd know one, if I saw one.'

'And you'd phone me?'

'Oh yes, Sir, night or day.'

'Good man, you've got the picture.'

Happer seemed cheered. The interview seemed at an end. That seemed to be that. But with great men you can never be sure. Suddenly Happer said in a lyrical tone (for a millionaire who was not talking about money): 'The northern sky is a very beautiful thing, Macintyre. You're going to have a wonderful trip.'

'Thank you, Sir.'

Assuming – and gratefully – that he had been dismissed from Happer's presence, Macintyre was passing Mrs Wyatt's desk on the return journey to the express elevator, when he heard Happer's voice.

'Macintosh.'

He thought he knew how St Peter felt the third time they came and asked that damn question. Except that at least they got Peter's name right (of course he wasn't a saint then, and not, on the whole, going the right way about becoming one), and Happer didn't. Except that, of course, Macintyre was no more his *real* name than Macintosh. He turned back.

'Sir?'

'Are you a married man?'

'No, Sir.' But then, anxious lest Happer should get the wrong impression, added: 'But I date girls.' (Which was a lie, since Trudi had moved out.)

'I'm not married either, but I used to date girls too.'

'Thank you, Sir.'

And as Macintyre retreated again past Mrs Wyatt's desk he heard behind him, like the roaring of a mad axeman, the word:

'Virgo!'

2

ABERDEEN

The petro-chemical capital of the free world

They had warned Danny Oldsen to be discreet. Danny, the local representative of Knox Oil and Gas, took the warning to heart. As the passengers from the Houston flight, connecting at Heathrow, disembogued through Gate 4 at Aberdeen Airport, he concealed beneath his coat the printed sign they had given him announcing 'Knox Oil and Gas', which was to serve as his introduction to Macintyre. What, thought Danny, what would Macintyre be like? Ah, if it were only one of those American lasses he was to meet, the sort you saw on the fillums with her shining hair and a letter from the name of her football team embroidered on her chest. 'Miss Macintyre, is it? May I call you Gloria?' And she would share her gum with him and take him off to meet Pop, who would look tired and concerned like Fred McMurray, and they would have a big wedding in Pop's front room, and all Miss Macintyre's friends would giggle at him, but secretly be madly jealous, until, in a hotel room overlooking Niagara Falls, she would take from her overnight case her diaphanous nightie, and standing in front of the window . . .

The trouble with Danny Oldsen's fantasies was that he never persisted with them to the really interesting bits. He would be *picked* to play for Rangers, or he would be lying second in the Olympic marathon with only a distressed Kenyan between him and the tape, or he would be sent for to Hollywood to do this screen test for the remake of *Gone With The Wind* – 'we want fresh young faces this time round, and we've scoured the world, but yours, Danny, is just so perfect, we felt we had to test you. But we ought to warn you that we are also testing Robert Redford, who has a controlling interest in the fillum, and therefore . . .'

In trying to be discreet, Danny had only succeeded in becoming the most remarked upon figure in the Aberdeen Airport concourse. At first Macintyre could not believe that this prancing creature was an employee of Knox Oil and Gas – he would certainly never have made it in Happer Tower, Houston – but when at length Danny allowed a few more inches of his printed sign to peep through his overcoat, Macintyre realized that it was, indeed, true.

'I didn't want to make a fuss,' Danny murmured intimately, fingering the sign under his coat. 'I know how delicate this whole business is. I suppose you can't tell me whether Fred McMurray has a daughter?'

'Do you have a car, Oldsen?'

'Sure.'

'And you'll take me to the laboratory?'

'Yeh.'

'Well, let's go.'

If Macintyre was disappointed in Oldsen's callow eccentricity, then Oldsen was equally disappointed in Macintyre, who did not appear old enough or stout enough to be important. If they had sent someone like Macintyre then they couldn't regard the project as being of top priority. Realizing that more was expected of him and that Macintyre was standing still in the centre of the Airport doing nothing, surrounded by cases, Oldsen said:

'Shall I give you a wee hand,' and pranced off with Macintyre's raincoat, leaving Macintyre to stagger after him with his baggage.

Why, Oldsen wondered when he and Macintyre reached the Knox Sea Laboratories, do they give scientists white coats to wear? Is it because they are half doctors and half madmen, or is it to dazzle the uninitiated? Scientists have power over life and death but no discernment as to what is right or wrong. They are the modern witches, but we don't hurt them; rather do they hurt us.

Geddes, head scientist at Knox Sea Laboratories, did not look like a witch, and nor did Watt, his familiar, who bustled about seeing to things. When Oldsen and Macintyre arrived at the laboratory, Watt was padding a small rubber boat around a topographical model of the Ferness bluff. Geddes continued to write things down on a clip-board, as though the clip-board and the portable computer-control that went with it were all that remained constant in a shifting world. He looked up tetchily when the oilmen came in.

'Did you close the door, you? This is a controlled environment.'

Watt added: 'We have moulting malacostracans in here. It's an exhausting and dangerous process. Too much natural light and they'll retreat into their shells – except that they don't have any right now. They're moulting, d'ye see?'

Macintyre made gestures to indicate that he had indeed closed the door; he looked quite crustacean as he paddled the air. Oldsen stepped on to the catwalk and made the introductions, at which Geddes welcomed them to his little world, and asked whether they would care for a trip round the bay. Before they could respond, they were joined on the catwalk by a young woman who wore her white coat with such a languorous air that it might have been a sheet, and she asleep under it. She had shades over her eyes and her light brown hair was tied in a bun on the top of her head. A faintly fishy smell wafted from her to Oldsen; he was smitten. He stared at her with such intensity that Geddes actually put down his clip-board and introduced the girl, whose name was Marina. So bemused was Macintyre by his jet-lag and the improbable environment in which he now found himself (everything in miniature after hours of looking at the world from a height of thirty-five thousand feet) that he hardly saw Marina. Marina seemed impervious to all of them. She smiled faintly. Geddes, jowly and serious, like a family grocer, said in an amiable enough way:

'We can simulate any sea conditions you care to mention – what would you like?'

Oldsen suggested 'A hurricane', and a look passed between Geddes and Watt. Glancing at the computer-control, Marina remarked:

'The sensor on forty-one's gone haywire. I'd better replace it,' with which she unfastened her bun and shook the hair loose, then removed the spectacles and the white coat to reveal a glistening body within a one-piece black swimsuit. With a glance at both the younger men she handed the coat and spectacles to Macintyre and dived into the water which parted to admit her so that there was scarcely a splash and hardly a ripple.

'Did you know,' Watt remarked, 'that the conger eel is one of the very few fishes without scales?'

'Is that so?' said Macintyre politely.

'Aye, and during their breeding season all their teeth fall out.'

'Enough of that, Norman,' Geddes said sharply, noting that his assistant was growing excited.

Meanwhile Marina had stayed under the water, her body just visible, as she made for the battery of sensors at the far end of the converted hangar. Mac and Danny were beginning to exhibit signs of anxiety when Watt reassured them:

'She's got a magnificent pair of lungs.'

'Oh yes,' said Geddes, 'she's a great asset. Five degrees in oceanography, and a very talented programme too.'

'Yes, very talented,' said Danny, thinking of an Esther Williams film he had once seen at the cinema in Peterhead.

'Good skin,' Mac added, feeling something was expected of him, 'good skin.' Evidently Danny was not satisfied with Mac's contribution for he grabbed the girl's coat from him and draped it over his own arm.

Said Geddes: 'I'll get rid of her when she surfaces. She's not in on this Ferness thing yet. Actually she's better in the field.' Watt nodded his agreement, as Marina broke the surface of the water below them, hair sleek around her head, eyes blinking. She placed a sensor at Geddes's feet and levered herself onto the catwalk.

'There's the dud.' She turned to Macintyre who grabbed her coat back from Danny and handed it to her. As she walked towards the offices, Danny gazed at her shoulder-blades and the hair tumbling like a torrent between them. For a moment she glanced back, possibly at all four men; she was still smiling. Danny was hopelessly in love.

'She's a good girl,' Watt remarked ambiguously, 'but things are still a bit hush hush. Well, I'll show you the site models now, shall I?'

'Aye, let you see what you're in the market for, Macintyre.'

As Geddes clambered around the hills and valleys of inland Ferness, Watt lifted out here the church and there a solitary farmstead; the cluster of cottages facing the sea lifted out in a single piece, revealing beneath it the storage tanks and power plants, the gantries and service jetties of the proposed terminal.

(In the village of Ferness on the other side of Scotland the inhabitants felt a tremor under their feet, as though the land itself was twitching in its sleep. In the Post Office and General Stores the tins of baked beans rattled on the shelves and Mrs Fraser looked nervously to see whether Rikki had driven his motor-bike into the wall again. The Reverend Murdo Mac-pherson in his modest Church considered whether divine enlightenment was imminent, or was it just a massive wave beating against the cliff? Gordon Urquhart, hotelier, tax-adviser, cab-driver, blamed the disturbance in the earth's equilibrium on the bombing of the neighbouring bay by the USAF jets. Gideon painting 'Bella Marguerita' on the prow of his fishing-boat saw the paintbrush jolt in his hand and the paint smudge, and blamed it on that extra dram of Glenmorangie at midday. Then the land settled again, and slumbered.)

Geddes was saying, as he handed the village to Mac: 'Oh, this is a bay in a million, the only one on the West Coast where the silt is deep enough for the foundation piles, and the harbour is a natural for blasting in the underground tanks.'

Watt caught his enthusiasm: 'Plus, you see, the debris rock will be used to fill in the other beach for the refinery. This place will become the petro-chemical capital of the free world.'

Geddes: 'Six months of blasting and two years for construction. I've worked out the stresses to the last PSI. This baby will last a thousand years . . . for ever . . . it'll even survive the next ice age – we've proved that you see, we've *proved* it. We've simulated ten thousand years of intense glaciation over the whole bay.'

'Not,' added Watt regretfully, 'not that we need that ice age. We could divert the Gulf Stream, take it up past Greenland (they would be grateful, those poor sons of bitches) and unfreeze the Arctic Circle. Geddes proved it right here, but they won't listen.'

'Thank you, Norman, but there was no need to bring that

up.' Geddes sounded like a dying man who had seen, snatched from his grasp and broken, the vial containing the secret of eternal youth. He sighed. It was a private moment.

'Will Marina be back?' asked Danny. He had not yet learned to live with disappointment.

'Not for a while,' said Geddes with indifference.

Mac, who was still holding Ferness in his arms like a large wedding cake, offered to return it to Geddes as he asked:

'Should we not be heading north soon? We'll see you when we get back maybe.'

'No, keep it, laddie, keep it,' said Geddes. 'Dream –' and he inhaled deeply – 'dream *large*.'

His dreams would never be fulfilled: the Arctic would never be unfrozen. Let younger men do what they could. All that was left to Geddes and Watt was a larger hangar filled with children's toys.

3

HEADING NORTH

Sure is a lot of scenery

Mac was car-sick; not sick in a car, but sick of a car and sick for a car. Danny Oldsen's driving was ingenuous: he would treat a straight stretch of road with exaggerated contempt, a twisty stretch of road with exaggerated caution. But even Mac would have been constrained by the tinny British box-on-wheels which was all, presumably, that Knox Oil and Gas, Aberdeen, reckoned Danny to be worth. Oh for his Porsche and a hundred miles of clearway, plus George Hamilton IV on the player and Trudi, compliant, scented, sweetly smiling by his side. Where was he driving her? To that fish restaurant on Highway 16, the one where you could choose your trout from a fish-tank and the Maitre D would bring it out in a gaffe. Instead of which he was sitting beside an overgrown adolescent driving jerkily through something called Fife, while the radio emitted an un-appetizing blend of bagpipes and static, and the possibility of getting a T-bone steak seemed as rare as the steak that might have been his at the Houston Chamber of Commerce Young Executives' Dinner. Plus the heater was blowing cold. Plus mist was descending. Plus he had missed the opportunity of a crap at Aberdeen airport, and that had been another mistake.

'What are you thinking about?' he asked Danny. What the hell *did* the guy think about?

'Girls,' said Oldsen. 'Naked girls.'

Instantly Trudi clambered back into Mac's imagination, her muscular thighs quivering. What was the Maitre D doing to her?

'Me too,' he muttered.

'In a fish-tank.'

'Yeah.' Mac was surprised. Surely to God Oldsen hadn't been to that place on Highway 16 or met Trudi.

'She was great,' Danny added.

'Who?'

'Marina, of course.'

'Oh. Yeah.'

In Danny's mind the fish-tank was scarcely large enough to contain Marina, who had to contort herself to keep swimming. What was great was that he, Danny, could walk around the fish-tank faster than Marina could swim around it, and yet Marina didn't seem to mind. She seemed quite to relish the hunt (if that was what it was) and smiled her enigmatic smile at him, as though the display were for his benefit alone.

They drove west, then they drove north, then they drove west. By the time the sun's rays had abandoned the lochs and the lower reaches of the glens for the crags where it gilded the wings of the golden eagles and set the heather alight for a few flamboyant minutes, Mac was asleep. He had been awake for twenty hours and had soared to thirty-five thousand feet and descended. He had gone east, then north, then west, then north, then west, until it seemed to him that it was he who was spinning, and the world which was standing still. Asleep, he looked young again. Ambition drained from his face, the draw-strings of self-protection which kept his lips tight and lined his cheeks were loosened, and he became chubby, a boy at peace. As the rays of the sun faded, so the glens grew heavy with moorland mist, and Danny, who no longer needed to shade his eyes, switched on the windscreen wipers, and leaned forward in his seat, shoulders hunched. In deference to Mac's exhaustion he had switched off the radio, but now he hummed gently to himself, something romantic, something he remembered from when he was first in love, a silly song about people growing old together and living on a hill. He hummed, and the mist rubbed itself against the windows like one of Eliot's cats, and then there was a thump, and Danny no longer hummed, and the car skidded to a halt, and Mac awoke.

'What's up?' he asked. He was completely bewildered, and knew neither where nor with whom he was; what he was, why he was, and, indeed, whether he was were deeper mysteries which would take longer to unravel.

Danny said: 'I think we hit something. It got misty all of a sudden, and I think we hit something.' He and the engine had stopped humming. The silence was total. He looked at Mac, awaiting orders. Danny was in the habit of running out of ideas very quickly. It was this which made him useful as a junior executive with Knox Oil and Gas, but would militate against his further promotion. So it was Mac who climbed out of the car first. As he did so the smell of Scottish mist and heather almost overwhelmed him. The two men walked through the mist with their arms outstretched, like men in blindfolds, but all that awaited them in the road was a rabbit, breathing heavily, placidly resentful.

'Aw, stuff!' said Danny, though relieved. 'I hate hitting things.'

'I think it's just kind of stunned,' said Mac, whose only previous acquaintance with rabbits had been at Playboy clubs.

'Mebbe it's broken its leg, or something? Shall we put it out of its misery?'

'What d'you mean?'

'Kill it,' Danny elaborated, 'hit it with something hard.'

'You've already done that with a two-ton automobile.' The logic was beyond argument. 'Just put it in the car.'

The presence of the terrified rabbit in the car made the men uneasy. Their tenuous relationship could not yet cope with strangers. The rabbit was like an unknown mourner at an intimate family funeral. The pall of mist grew ever thicker, the cold colder.

'Well, we can't drive in this stuff,' said Danny.

'Where are we?'

It was evident that Danny didn't know where they were. Mac cursed his luck that he, a Telex man, should have been selected for such a trip. It was not the first time that he had cursed it.

'The last couple of road signs were in Gaelic – it's not one of my languages.'

'You speak languages?' Mac was intrigued to find that Oldsen had a talent for something, however useless.

'French, Italian, Spanish,' said Danny, pausing for effect before continuing, 'Greek, Turkish, Russian, Swedish, German, Japanese, Dutch and Polish ... I have a facility with languages.'

'Can you say anything interesting in any of them?'

'I don't know what you mean.' Danny glanced sidelong at Mac, before continuing: 'Je ne comprends pas. Non comprendo. No comprendi. No capito.'

Mac had been fishing in the pockets of his jacket. 'I've got some chocolate and two packets of Pan American Coffeemate. What've you got?'

Predictably Danny said: 'Nothing,' but continued: 'Rien. Niente. Nada.'

'OK. OK.'

In the gloom of the car six eyes shone white, like pebbles

34

under water or stars in the sky. Chocolate was distributed, but not to the rabbit. Hunting through his pockets, Mac had remembered something. Now he produced from his wallet a photograph which he passed to Danny.

'This is my car. A Porsche 9 3 0 turbo-charged.' Danny was impressed. 'A good car is important. I used to get migraine headaches when I drove a Chevvy. A car like mine won't let you down.' He remembered some copy from a *Playboy* ad. 'There's only two things better than a German car – that's a Swiss watch and a woman from anywhere.' In the middle of a Scottish glen the remark sounded vacuous, although Danny seemed to be giving serious thought to it. Or maybe he was merely translating it into Polish. Mac decided not to share any more chocolate. He would eat the rest when Danny was asleep.

Suddenly, and to the rabbit's concern, the alarm of Mac's digital watch played the first four bars of the 'Yellow Rose of Texas'.

'Conference Time in Texas.' Astonishingly Mac felt homesick for Happer Tower. 'I'll give them a call tomorrow.'

Danny said: 'Good night,' and closed his eyes. He was asleep almost at once.

'Yeh, good night.'

Mac was thinking of Happer and Cal Wrain, of Angela and Trudi, of Geddes and Watt, of Danny and the rabbit. He imagined all of them as a basketball team. What kind of shorts would Happer wear? What use would the rabbit be? He would devise a match for them, and the opponents could be either country singers – Dolly Parton, yeh! – or American presidents. Roosevelt would be a problem. The referee was Burt Lancaster. He was most authoritative. Just as Burt was blowing his whistle, Mac, who was the sportscaster, heard his watch alarm once more. It was morning.

Danny was also woken by the alarm. The rabbit, to judge from its wide, omniscient eyes, had watched all night. Both men were cold and stiff, hungry and disorientated. Mac limped out of the car and, aware of Danny watching, started the sequence of exercises employed by the US marines to lick the rookies into shape. Danny relieved himself in a ditch. The mist had lifted. As soon as Mac was fit to join the marines (though his crumped oilman's suit was incongruous) he looked up and saw a tall monument at the head of a spectacularly beautiful loch. On the monument a figure, proud and erect.

'Hi,' said Danny, picking leaves for the rabbit's breakfast.

'Yeh. Who's that guy?'

Danny crossed the road to where there was a board with writing on it. Soon he was an authority. The Glenfinnan monument commemorated the Gathering of the Clans, and the man was Prince Charlie. Mac considered the matter.

'He was fighting against the English?'

'He was.'

'Us too. Who was king at the time? George?'

'There wasn't a king. It was Cromwell.'

'What was he, a president?'

'I suppose. In a way.'

'I thought the English had kings or queens.'

'It was a while ago.'

'Who won?'

Danny found that hard to answer. He talked of Culloden. Mac looked around him at the rocky outcrops, some of which were extinct volcanoes, smoothed down by a couple of ice ages. It was an old landscape, older than Knox Oil, older than the oil itself.

'There sure is a lot of history round here.'

As though the sky were being torn apart, two jet fighter bombers streaked over Glenfinnan, no more than a hundred feet above the water of the loch, which was shadowed by their passing. Mac and Oldsen ducked. Before they had time to raise their heads, the aircraft had vanished behind the hills, the noise lingering for a few seconds, as a concert hall vibrates at the end of a symphony.

'We're way off our route,' said Danny. 'We'd best get going.' Even so he insisted on feeding the rabbit before resuming the journey.

'Think I'll call him Harry,' he said.

'Her name's Trudi.'

Caring nothing about its name, the hermaphrodite rabbit chewed contentedly on its grass and docken leaves.

'I'll drive,' said Mac, 'you can navigate.'

'I'm hungry,' said Danny.

Mac felt in his pockets and found the remains of the chocolate. Its silver paper had become detached, and it was covered in lint. Neither of them fancied it.

'Sure is a lot of scenery too,' said Mac, as he drove north into it. Three hours later they reached Ferness.

4

FERNESS

The only business

Mornings varied little in Ferness. The tide was high or low, the sea rough or calm, the weather wet or fine, the barometer rising or falling. Either there were lobsters in the creels or crabs; usually both, occasionally neither, in which case the rich businessmen in the big hotels in Fort William, Inverness and London slavered in vain. Sometimes visitors checked in at the Macaskill Arms; a location hunter from a film company, or a man from Edinburgh checking that Ferness had not been pulled down – for it was on a list of protected Scottish villages – or a solitary rock climber or an ornithologist in search of the red-throated diver or the Slavonian grebe or the black guillemot or 'tystie' (which looks as though its shirt is hanging out). Your actual tourists seldom ventured down the absurdly steep and twisting hill which was the only route into (or out of) the village; the rewards for risking the descent scarcely justified the effort, for there were no trips around the bay, no shops selling buckets and spades, no gourmet restaurants (although Stella Urquhart cooked a formidable French onion soup) or fish-and-chip bars, nothing, in short, to make life worth living for those whose lives are not worth living without such pleasures.

The people of Ferness were not unwelcoming but they had their own lives to lead. Rikki had his motor-bike and Murdo Macpherson his Church on the cliffs; Gideon his paint-pot and Roddy his investments; Edward and Peter their boats and young Iain his collection of matchbox labels; Mrs Fraser her general stores and her CB radio and Gordon and Stella the Macaskill Arms and one another. Sometimes a sign would be posted on the jetty that the Ferness Leisure and Athletic Committee, under Roddy's chairmanship, would be holding a whist-drive, or that an evening's entertainment was to be provided by a local fiddle and accordion band. Sometimes Ben, from his shack on the beach, would report that a consignment of door handles or cannabis resin or bicycle pumps had been washed up, and an impromptu sale would be held; and at irregular intervals Victor Pinochkin, Russian trawlerman and putative father of numerous progeny around the Western approaches, would come ashore; but for the most part life in Ferness could be depended upon to follow a predictable course, unless and until Mac and Danny drove down the hill with a model of the village in the boot and an injured rabbit on the back seat.

There was only one street. It divided the houses from the beach. The white stone houses with their sloping roofs clustered together around the hotel and its bar, as a family around its breadwinner. Within the harbour the creel boats bobbed, and within the hotel Gordon and Stella Urquhart lay together and giggled at the absurdity of existence and the incidental pleasures that lay along the primrose path.

Mac and Danny drove along the one street until halted by a black dog lying stretched out in front of the car. With exquisite slowness the dog stirred itself and staggered to the side of the road.

'Some place,' Mac muttered bitterly. He parked the car and rattled the door of the hotel. It appeared to be locked. Danny banged the knocker. Gordon's face appeared at a first-floor window; it was, thought Mac, a rather insulting sort of face. Behind him, and much more to Mac's taste, appeared Stella.

'What is it?'

Mac said: 'Sorry to trouble you so early . . . we'd like to check in, and maybe eat something.'

'Breakfast isn't until eight – seven in the fishing season. It's not the fishing season.'

'Could we check in anyway? We've been on the road all night. We have an injured rabbit also.'

Gordon's face removed itself from the window, leaving Stella's mounted and framed within the aperture. She glanced at Danny, then focused on Mac, raising an eyebrow and smiling. Gordon appeared at the door, tightening the cord of his robe.

'It was never locked.' He led them to the kitchen. 'Are you passing through?'

'We might stay for a few days,' said Mac. How the hell did you pass through a place with only one access road, he wondered. But the kitchen surprised him. It was modern, well appointed, and the fridge-freezer would not have looked out of place in Houston.

'Why don't you make yourselves some toast and coffee – we can take care of the formalities later.' He smiled pleasantly at his two guests. 'I have to go back upstairs just now. There's some lettuce in the fridge for the rabbit.'

'What the hell is a fridge?' Mac asked, but Oldsen seemed at home in the kitchen.

'Nice people,' he said.

'Yeh. And they speak English.'

A wistful look crossed Danny's face. 'Hey, do you think they're at it up there?'

'No,' said Mac, as though determined to stop them if they

were. Long journeys tended to make him horny, and lack of sleep had the same effect, and he had been stuck in an under-sized British car with a Polish-speaking moron and a twitching rabbit. But despite Mac's strenuous denial, both men moved silently around the kitchen preparing breakfast and straining to hear a creak or a sigh, a giggle or a moan.

Upstairs, Gordon and Stella were more relaxed. Curiously the idea of the two exhausted men downstairs intrigued Stella, whose brown wavy hair washed against the pillow like the tide.

'We have an injured rabbit also,' said Gordon mockingly in a camp American voice.

'Do you think it's them?' Stella undid the buttons of Gordon's Viyella pyjamas, but without the urgency of a newly-wed. She was coming home to anchor, riding with the tide. Gordon was absolutely certain that it was 'them'; what other business could two young executives have in Ferness so early in the morning of a day in late spring?

'Christmas,' said Gordon, easing one arm out of his pyjama, 'might be early this year.'

'What do you want for Christmas?' Stella wanted to know. She was in a generous mood.

'We might get that new mattress.'

There was giggling and then some playful kissing, which soon turned more serious, the way kissing will when time is short, and then a knock at the door. Again Stella giggled, for the knock had come at a bad moment for Gordon. He was prepared to be quite abrupt with whichever of the two men it was who needed attending to (there were no other guests in the hotel), until he heard the gist of Mac's request – for it was Mac. Mac needed – Gordon had to concentrate to get this right – he needed an *adaptor* so that he could *plug in* his *briefcase* which had an electric lock, of all things, whose battery needed recharging. Gordon knew how the battery felt. From the bed Stella laughed happily, not caring who heard her.

'Leave it to me,' said Gordon, uncharacteristically lost for an answer, but Macintyre would not. A fool and his briefcase, thought Mac, were soon parted. He wondered whether Stella was sitting up in bed, and, if so, what she was wearing, and he stared at the intervening door as though his laser-beam eyes could burn holes in it; but they couldn't. Defeated, he returned down the corridor, pursued by Stella's laughter.

He spent the morning unpacking. It was the pleasantest way Mac could imagine to spend a morning – almost. It was not a chore so much as a duty, and not a duty so much as a ritual. Before he could unpack he had to make sure that his face was shaved and his hands completely clean. He was proud of his hands. He had once read in *Playboy* the opinion that since your hand was what you offered first to a new acquaintance, your hand was what he or she first judged you on, and initial impressions, of course, were all important. Mac had taken this to heart, and his handshake was not only frank and virile and trustworthy, but the most wholesome in Texas. Certainly the clothes in his suitcase deserved no better. The coolness of the pigskin, the tact of the zip, the way the clothes lay folded in neat patterns like the order beds of some ancient physic garden, it was a journey through an exotic country, this unpacking of the cases. He hung up the suits outside the wardrobe, of whose mustiness he was suspicious, and patted their arms into shape. He placed tissue-paper between the shirts. By the time he had finished it was almost lunch-time. Despite the euphoria brought on by the unpacking, he was conscious of something lacking. What was it? His watch was on his wrist, his toiletries in the mirrored cupboard above the basin, whose water he was surprised to find was pleasantly hot, and all was as it should be, except . . . Then he realized that for the first time in his life he was to sleep in a room without a telephone.

*

Lunch in the modest, low-ceilinged dining-room was served by Gordon Urquhart. Gordon had rolled up his sleeves and tied an apron around his waist, but it still failed to make him a waiter. His obsequiousness was tinged with irony, was *almost* insolent.

'Everything OK gents?' he asked as he cleared away the remains of their grilled sardines. 'We do a hot lunch every other day . . . so you were lucky.'

Said Macintyre: 'We have to talk to a Mr Urkyheart, an accountant, I believe. Can you tell me where we might find him?'

Gordon smiled and said in his best Kelvin Academy tone of voice: 'Indeed yes . . . he has an office next door, to the left, on the first floor, and I happen to know that he'll be there in about fifteen minutes.'

'Thank you. Delicious. Compliments to the, um, chef.'

Although the office was next door to the hotel the two oilmen had an eventful journey. As they stepped into the road Rikki chanced by on his motor-bike, orange helmet over his eyes and greenish smoke pouring from his exhaust. Then they were greeted cheerily by Gideon, the aged painter of aged boats, who was bestowing the name 'Bella Marguerita' on the prow of Roddy's vessel. It was generally understood that although the Ferness boat owners could not afford new boats, it helped their morale if, during the off-season, Gideon gave their boats new names. They were less aware of the man on the roof of the Macaskill Arms who, while ostensibly replacing tiles, could see directly into Gordon Urquhart's accountancy office.

Gordon had replaced his waiter's shirt, cardigan and apron with a lightweight grey suit. His hair was brushed back from his forehead where before it had been casually tousled. Danny was convinced that he could see shreds of grey glistening in it where fifteen minutes ago it had been badger black. Certainly Gordon the accountant looked ten years older, and a great deal wiser, than Gordon the waiter.

The oilmen were welcomed into his small office and their surprise at finding the hotelier doing duty as a chartered accountant was soon allayed as Gordon explained that in Ferness it was the fashion to double up on jobs – he was not only hotel manager and accountant but sometimes taxi-driver as well. 'And now, gentlemen,' he concluded, 'what can I do for you?'

Macintyre dredged up a smile. 'I represent Knox Oil and Gas, Mr Urkyheart –'

'Gordon –' and Gordon looked encouraging.

'OK, Gordon, and I believe that some of my people let you know that we would be calling.'

'That's right. So what's up?'

'Well, we're in the business of acquiring some real estate in the area. We want to ask for your help in co-ordinating our work.'

'What do you want to buy?'

Macintyre paused for a moment. An image of the rabbit on the seat of the car twitched into his mind, and broke his concentration. He blanked it out, and continued:

'I won't be coy with you, Gordon: we want to buy the whole place. We want to buy everything from the cliffs to the north right through to the bay on the far side and we want to go about a mile inland too; that's all.'

Urquhart was stunned. He was also excited. This was not to be merely a matter of new mattresses, that much was obvious. But he kept his accountant's face on.

'You're talking about fifteen, maybe twenty properties, families, businesses, farms. You're talking about a lot of money.'

Mac smiled the smile of someone who has money to spend. 'I don't think we have to go into figures right now. I have a breakdown of the properties and I think it's a matter of bringing the community together, making a collective deal if you like.'

He might have money, Gordon thought, and those he represented certainly seemed keen to do a deal; in such circumstances the financial wizard can afford to play for time. Evidently it was a seller's market, and the buyers were not going to pull out. Who were the richest people in the world just now? Why, American oilmen. And what happened when the richest people in the world wanted something real bad?

'Why don't you get to know the place? Spend a few days? I'll take things just as far as I can, gentlemen, and get back to you. How about it?'

'OK Gordon, if you think it will take that long.'

Gordon narrowed his eyes. 'Are you talking about the Church too?'

'Yes.'

'Well now, that's going to be tricky. The Church, do you see, has very definite views about property.'

'We'll leave it with you anyway, OK?'

Mac rose from his chair: Danny did the same. Until this meeting Danny had not entirely understood all that was involved in the deal. He thought of the men in the Marine Research Laboratory in Aberdeen taking hold of Ferness and lifting it out of Scotland; to them it had been a toy: to Mac it was an opportunity to shine: to Knox Oil and Gas it was, or soon would be, a processing plant and an oil terminal. So what was it to the folk who lived there? And what was it to him, Danny? The earth is the Lord's, and the fullness thereof. And when the Pope visited a country he kissed the ground. Once this land had belonged to the Norse gods, so many gods to be placated; gods of rivers and trees, gods of the sky and the sea. With so many gods one had to tread carefully, one had to bargain, one had to decide whether to please a powerful one at the risk of offending two weaker ones. With just the one God, things were easier. Och, He couldn't keep an eye on *everything*. And so the hedgerows were burnt, and the trees cut down; the wild flowers sprayed and the sky polluted. The old gods were powerless to stop it – they had been victims of a massive take-over, had received their golden handshakes, had gone into re-tirement, and the new God was a multinational; He had a finger in every pie, but did anyone still believe that He cared that much for the fall of a sparrow?

Gordon was recommending that they took in the beach, relaxed for a while. It was a beautiful place, he said, and he promised to prepare some figures. He seemed pleased. Mac seemed pleased. Neither apparently shared his, Danny's, unease.

Alone in his office, Gordon shuffled his feet ecstatically on the floor, until the boards creaked. The shuffle became a dance, the dance a song. 'Take it away, Andrew!' he cried. He grinned, he waved his arms around, he hugged himself. 'Oh boy,' was the chorus, 'are we going to be rich!'

> 'Oh Mr Macintyre, I adore you,
> Oh Mr Macintyre, you love me too,
> I know you do.'

'Hey Stella,' he cried (for what's in a chorus if you have to sing it solo?), 'hey Stella, Stella!'

A happy man. But, as the Greeks knew, one should call no man happy until he dies. The Norse gods knew this too.

After dinner Macintyre and Danny followed Gordon's advice, and strolled on the beach. The sun seemed particularly reluctant to abandon Ferness; it rolled around the horizon until the men grew giddy watching it. The glow of the sunset singed the surf and the sea-birds caught between the incandescent sky and the ignited sea appeared like mythical creatures, immortal and pos-sessed of ineffable powers. Even a ringed plover paddling inele-gantly in the wet sand and an oyster-catcher pecking at a shell seemed part of a mysterious ritual which Mac and Danny could only watch and wonder at. The keening of the gulls and the gentle hissing of the waves lulled and soothed them, and Mac would have been happy to walk along the fringe of the surf until morning; but Danny, inoculated from childhood against these marine infections, broke the mood.

'What do you make of Urquhart?'

'He smelled the money.'

Danny considered the smell of money and compared it to the smell of seaweed. 'It's a nice beach,' he said.

Said Mac: 'We should come here when we have to talk business. The hotel is too public.'

'Right.'

Some distance away, where the dunes gave shelter to the beach, they could just make out a tumbledown structure of canvas, jetsam and corrugated iron from which rose a thin stream of smoke. They stopped walking and turned away from the sea. Danny pointed towards some low cliffs.

'That's where the jetty will be . . . and the storage tanks over here, all the way up the beach. It's just like the model.'

'More expensive,' Mac muttered.

'Way out there,' said Danny and pointed at the efflorescent sea, 'the pipeline terminal will just about join the two sides of the bay.'

'Where we are,' Mac said, 'must be where the pumping station will be.'

'Aye,' and Danny sighed with the grandeur of it all, 'it's some business.'

They turned and walked back along the shore. The footprints of their first journey had already been obliterated. Now that the spell had been broken Mac spoke with great enthusiasm:

'It's the only business. Can you imagine a world without oil? No automobiles, no paint, no polish, no ink –'

'No Nylon –'

'No detergents –'

'And Perspex. No Perspex.'

'No Polythene –'

'And no dry-cleaning fluid –'

'No waterproof coats. Hey, do they really make dry-cleaning fluid out of petroleum?'

'Yeh. Sure they do.'

'I didn't know that.' Mac tried to imagine a world without dry-cleaning fluid and found it remarkably easy.

Danny heard a loud kerplomp and spun round in time to see widening ripples in the shallows. A seal? Or if not a seal . . .? He glanced at Mac, but Mac had heard nothing.

'You know anything about the stars?' he inquired of Danny.

'I recognize that one.' And Danny nodded familiarly at the only star yet visible. 'It's the evening star. I think it's Venus.'

'Is that the same as the morning star?'

'It depends on your point of view.'

'Yes, but is it the same star?'

'The morning star *is* the evening star.' Danny tested it on his tongue. The logic of it bothered him.

'I'll have to get a book,' said Mac. 'There are things I need to check out.'

They had reached a low barrier of rocks and were about to negotiate them when Mac's digital alarm clock played a snatch of 'The Yellow Rose of Texas'. The sequence of notes sounded paltry against the gulls and the surf; it was entirely without resonance.

'Conference time in Houston. I shall have to make some calls.' And they both turned towards the lights of the village which, though few in number, seemed suddenly welcoming and safe.

Until the light failed, Stella had watched the two men from the window of her room in the hotel. She had watched how at first they had walked quickly along the strand, keeping safely out of reach of the surf and glancing at one another as they talked, then how they had reduced their pace, and looked about them, and seemed more at ease. The taller of the two, Danny, held little interest for her. He was a type she knew well, a young and ambitious sort who would run with the English hare and hunt with the American hounds, not unlike Gordon, except that Gordon lived by his own peculiar set of moral absolutes, which may have been obscure to others, but were plain enough to him. Och, she could deal with a hotel full of Dannys. Macintyre though did interest her; he of the absurd electrical briefcase and beautiful clothes. She had been into his room – ostensibly to air and dust the place – and had been amazed by the beauty of his suits and shirts. He had monograms on his underwear, which was silk, and his pyjamas were from a superior culture to Gordon's stripy things. Not that she was dissatisfied with or bored by Gordon; quite the contrary; she loved him dearly. But Americans were special – and Gordon thought so too, which gave her the excuse she needed to run her fingers inside the elastic of his seductive underpants and to stare wistfully at him from hotel bedrooms. Because she also knew that he was absurd, and powerful, and away from home.

In the evenings the bar of the Macaskill Arms became the centre of the community. Whisky settled all differences, and, when it had done so, uncovered a few more. Mac and Danny approached the bar, behind which Roddy in his traditional cowboy shirt was serving. Mac inquired whether there was a telephone he could use, and Roddy remarked with justifiable pride that on the jetty there was a telephone-box from which you could speak to anywhere in the world. But Danny pointed out that, while this was theoretically true, he would in practice need some 10p pieces. As a Telex man, born and bred, Mac was fazed by this, so Danny produced a five pound note, and Roddy, unable to find fifty 10p's in the till, addressed the crowded bar:

'Any tens, lads? The gentleman here wants to make a very

important long distance phone call – intercontinental – so give me all your tens, lads.'

At once Danny and Mac were surrounded by a cluster of Ferness inhabitants, eager, indeed almost desperate, to be of assistance. It was a relief to Mac to escape from the bar with his coins, or would have been had not Rikki chosen that moment to roar past on his insatiable motor-bike.

'Aye, Rikki's on the road tonight,' said Iain, a plump, bearded young fisherman, in a doom-laden voice. He had followed Mac out of the bar; 'you need to look both ways when Rikki's about.'

The advice, thought Mac, would have been superfluous had he emerged a second sooner. In the event it was too late to be useful. But Iain seemed particularly keen to be of service, and shepherded Mac to the phone-box, holding open the door, from whose glass he removed a stain, rubbing it vigorously with his elbow. But Mac was not aware of any servility. The lad handed the receiver to him, and then grabbed it back, wiping the mouthpiece with a clean handkerchief.

'Here we are, Mr Mac. Full working order.' And indeed the Texan was surprised to find that the booth was both clean and well maintained, free of graffiti and with an impressive pile of directories. Plus the light worked.

'Thanks. I'm fine now. Thank you.' But still the young fellow was reluctant to leave.

'You have the proper code? Or will I get the operator for you?' And so on. It took all Mac's powers of persuasion before he could get Iain to realize that his continued presence was neither necessary nor welcome. Even then he hovered for a while around the booth, like a child who believes that if he leaves the room his new toy may disappear, or a politician who has long outlived his usefulness but refuses to accept that the world will continue to spin without his nudging it.

At last Mac was left in peace, feeding 10p's into a coin box while all around him the night sky throbbed with stars.

5

HOUSTON

The star-patient

The sky and the stars were excluded from Happer Tower, Happer Plaza, Houston. Even with ID cards and security clearance, they would not have been welcomed. One cannot feed the infinite into a computer, nor can one budget for Qazars or Black Holes. Nor was there ever darkness in Happer Tower. Knox Oil and Gas, said the commercials, Illuminate the World. The building hummed with static electricity and some of the newest recruits, who had not yet got around to having their shoes treated, could get quite a severe shock were they rash enough to shake hands with one another. The switchboard operators at the central exchange kept their feet off the ground, resting them on chromium bars beneath their stools. They were handsome girls, chosen by the personnel manager, whose probity was unquestioned – he was Happer's nephew, but they sat with their ears covered under neon strips, repeating, as caged birds repeat, the one phrase which they had been taught to say. 'Thank you for calling, Knox Oil and Gas.' In their plumage, and in the tragedy of their impoverished expectations, they resembled caged birds. No wonder they pecked at their food, no wonder they suffered from fallen arches, constipation, missed periods, halitosis, acne, allergies, scurvy and insanity. 'Thank you for calling, Knox Oil and Gas.' One girl, less willing than the rest to settle for the cage and the meaningless insincere rigmarole, had varied it, saying one day: 'Thank you for balling me, go home and piss,' and the next: 'Think you're appalling, cocks on the grass,' and so on. Nobody reported her for, to tell the truth, nobody cared what the girls said, and she tired of her small revolution long before it was noticed.

However, to Mac in his box in the middle of the sky, the bright chirrups of the gaily plumed birds created in him a pang of homesickness for which he was entirely unprepared.

'OK, OK,' he blurted out,' 'just get me Mr Cal Wrain, of Negotiations, willya, and hurry, please. I'm speaking from a very great distance.'

Cal sounded pleased to hear him, if rather surprised at the urgency in Mac's voice, as Mac gave him the number of the Ferness call-box, and begged to know how things were.

'Just the same, Mac – it's only been a coupla days.'

'It seems longer than that. I feel as if I've been here for ever.'

'Take it easy, Mac. How's the deal?'

'It might take a little time. Hey there's a nice beach here, Cal.' He was interrupted by the pips and fed more coins into the slot. The guy sounds a little crazy, Cal thought, when he resumed: 'Cal, you've got the number, huh? Well keep in touch, man, Ferness 261, yeh, I'll do the same.'

'Sure, I have the number. Keep at it Mac; just spend the money, OK?' Cal was ready with more helpful advice as soon as this batch had traversed the Atlantic, but the line went dead. Mac was left in the bright red booth, alone, quiet, with the darkness all around. As he pushed the door open, he could smell the seaweed, hear the surf and the gulls, feel the breeze. The stars dazzled him. The darkness lay on him so weightily it seemed as if his neck might break. He dragged in mouthfuls of air. He put one hand out to touch the night. He saw Houston diminish to the proportions of a doll's house, and then rush off into the void. He turned around slowly. Something was happening to him, something he could not control.

From a window in the hotel Stella could see him outlined against the telephone-box. She felt so sorry for him she could hardly bear it, but then, as suddenly, her sympathy was replaced by anger. What right had he to meddle with her in this way? She just hoped Gordon knew what he was doing.

The cries of the birds grew louder, the stars grew brighter, and Mac staggered towards the hotel.

According to Moritz the analysis was proceeding satisfactorily; according to Happer it could only be called satisfactory in the sense that it is satisfactory when an old car is reduced to a tiny cube of scrap metal. When Happer complained that Moritz was a fink, Moritz beamed; the omens were good; transference was taking place. When Happer shouted that he had never wanted to sleep with his mother, Moritz laughed and wagged a finger at him and called him playful. And when Happer insisted that he was being destroyed, Moritz agreed, expressed his approval and announced that they were ready to move on to the next stage. Happer seemed alarmed and wanted to know in what way the *next* stage would be an advance on *previous* stages. Moritz said that they would start to physicalize things a little.

'What?'

'I could hit you, Happer, wouldn't that humiliate you? Doggone it man, of course it would. We could progress by leaps and bounds. I could tie you up for starters.' Happer was shocked and affronted at the suggestion. One did not need an analyst to dish out that sort of dirt.

'Forget it, Moritz, you're talking about perversion, not therapy. Get out *now*, and don't come back.'

Moritz hopped about in delight. 'That's good! You're reacting . . . you're upset already. Think what it will be like when I punch you!'

Happer stood up. He was taller than Moritz and in better shape.

'Get out,' he warned, 'before *I* punch *you*.' Still beaming and paddling the air with his flippers, Moritz backed towards the door which, being electronically operated from Happer's desk, was already open.

'This is most gratifying, Mr Happer. It vindicates my entire therapy, the whole programme. I have your ego on the run, Mr Happer, you *piece of shit*' – this delivered with sudden venom – 'er, sorry, Sir, that just slipped out. You'll be hearing from me. We can't give up now. You're a star patient, Mr Happer.'

Just as his gesticulating figure was about to be lost to view behind the door, Moritz's head bobbed back: 'I might have to raise my fee when we do get physical, Mr Happer, but it won't be anything unreasonable. Good afternoon.' No sooner was the analyst gone than Happer pressed the intercom button.

'Mrs Wyatt, cancel all future appointments with Moritz – yes, all – and get me Hawaii on the phone. I want Fisher at the Observatory.'

6

FERNESS

Spoiling a very nice area

Macintyre's life at Ferness had become triangular. He felt himself shunted from bedroom to dining-room, from dining-room to beach. In the bedroom, Trudi lived; she seemed – or so Mac fancied – to welcome him into the room. But he always felt not that she had been put into his charge so much as that he had been put into hers.

He never saw her sleep. He would wake in the night and see through the darkness those darned white eyes, wide and watchful. He became embarrassed to undress in front of her. Through the walls he could hear the murmur of Stella's and Gordon's voices, and their laughter. They had each other, and he, the Playboy, had the rabbit.

In the dining-room Gordon was in charge. As a waiter he was exemplary. The food was served quietly and respectfully and removed with the merest hint of a flourish. But his presence in this subservient role made it impossible for Mac to discuss the purpose of their visit to Ferness, and they had little else in common. So, to the accompaniment of cheap Musack and blended wines, they acted out the rigmarole of polite banalities, and thought their own thoughts.

On the beach Mac and Danny could talk, but although they could not be eavesdropped upon there, they found it hard to concentrate on the matters in hand, and spoke instead of shells and seaweed, of fish and birds. Once they spotted some stocky birds, plumed black and brown and white, pecking at pebbles. They were turnstones. Mac was worried that they might get wet, but Danny assured him that they were waterproofed, whereat Mac looked at him and them with new respect. Sometimes they saw in the sky four white lines approaching from the South. These were jet-streams from a jet bomber which passed low over their heads at great speed and silently. The awesome scream of its engine pursued it as it dipped below the cliffs to the north, dropping its load of bombs into the neighbouring beach. Thuds and puffs of smoke indicated that its mission had been accomplished. These jets became familiar objects to the two men who, after a few such sorties, omitted to duck their heads and peer anxiously upwards. Sometimes the jet bombers came in pairs, occasionally even in threes or fours; usually they bombed the beach. Once Danny tried waving at one, but Mac told him not to bother. Travelling at such speed the pilot would not be able to appreciate these friendly gestures.

'Do you suppose he despises us?' Danny asked.

'He's just doing his duty,' said Mac.

On several occasions they observed outside the shack on the beach the figure of an elderly man. He might be digging around in a patch of seaweed, or whittling a stick, or sucking a pipe. Once he waved at them. Resenting this, Danny called him a crazy old man.

On the fourth day, Mac suggested they check out the Church and talk to the Minister. He felt he owed it to Happer to initiate a dialogue with somebody, and Urquhart had indicated that the Church might be the toughest nut to crack. Danny Oldsen agreed, but he seemed vague and abstracted. Mac asked him what was wrong.

'Do you think Gordon and Stella do it every night?' Mac paused for a moment, recalling the sighs and the giggles, and Stella in her long white nightdress at the end of the narrow corridor.

'Of course not,' he replied angrily.

Since the bar of the Macaskill Arms ministered to the spiritual needs of the villagers, it would be logical to suppose that the Church ministered to the secular; logical and true. Never having had a religious vocation, the Reverend Murdo Macpherson, an African, was welcomed in a village where they did not require such abstract qualities in their preacher. Murdo had come to Ferness as a student Minister, had liked the place which reminded him of the Cameroons, had shot a 75 at his first attempt on the links, and had stayed. He smiled throughout baptisms and funerals, but kept a solemn face for weddings; delivered his sermons, which were usually about golf and the parable of the Talents, in a sonorous voice, and was a ready touch when times got rough. What more could one require of a Minister?

On the morning when Macintyre and Danny Oldsen decided to visit the Church, the Church was already filled with the entire population of the village, and it was not in a reverential mood. The joint, in brief, was jumping. Urquhart was in the pulpit trying to calm the loudest mouths, while Murdo was standing at the foot of the pulpit, smiling benignly. The joint was jumping because Gordon had just implied that it was only a matter of days before they were all richer than they had ever dared to dream.

'Quiet please, everyone!' cried Murdo.

When the hubbub had diminished sufficiently to enable Gordon to be heard, he told them that they were a wee bit previous; nobody had yet mentioned money; all he needed at the moment was a general mandate from the villagers to negotiate on their behalf.

'I've got the Knox man on the hook – just give me the time to land him in style. He's got a bag full of money – stay calm now – I need your patience and your faith . . . trust me.'

Old Gideon, the boat-painter, in an antique Aran jersey, stood up and asked, his voice quavering: 'Do they want to buy a boat too, Mr Urquhart?'

'Gideon, if things go well they'll have to buy their own shirts back off us this time next week – now stay calm.'

The Reverend Macpherson, overcome by seeing his Church full for the first time since he came to Ferness twelve years prior to these events, announced that a short prayer would be appropriate, and Gordon agreed. The Reverend Macpherson raised his arms, turned the pink of his hands to bless the congregation and had just invoked the name of the Lord, when Roddy burst into the Church through the main door.

'The Yank and the other one! They're coming across to the Church! I saw them!'

'Oh God,' cried Murdo instinctively.

From the pulpit Gordon took charge. Everyone was to be silent; everyone was to keep still. And Murdo was to go out like what's-his-name in that film called whatever-it-was and deal with them. Murdo had never seen himself in a heroic role before. He wondered whether to pray to the Lord to take this cup from his lips, but there was not really time for a miracle. Macintyre and Danny were already in the churchyard.

'Not a sound now,' said the local hero, and thrust open the Church doors.

The Church squatted on a low eminence to the north of the beach and around it was a small graveyard. The dead lay huddled together, presumably from fellowship, for, had they wanted to spread themselves, there was most of North-West

Scotland to do it in. Mac and Danny read some of the head-
stones. On one stone would be carved four generations of a
single family. Children died, survived by their grandparents;
brothers were drowned in the same storm; mothers died in
childbirth; fathers in the wars. Some of the epitaphs were in
Gaelic. Macintyre noticed that several of the stones commemorated folk called Knox.

'You don't think . . .?' he began.

'Och no, it's a common enough name hereabouts,' Danny
answered.

Forcing an amiable smile onto his handsome features, the
Reverend Murdo Macpherson strode towards them in the sunshine. Instead of a sheriff's star he wore a dog-collar. His voice
was deep as the African jungle and wild as a Scottish moor.
Macintyre had some difficulty in understanding what he said.

'Good morning, gentlemen. Can I help you?'

'Reverend Macpherson? My name's Macintyre.'

'You're not Scottish, are you?'

'I'm American actually.'

Relieved to have discovered common ground with Macintyre
so quickly, Murdo said: 'I'm not a Scotsman either. I'm an
African.'

Politely Mac and Danny feigned surprise. 'I came here as a
student Minister and didn't ever get away again. Now what
can I do for you?'

'We're here on a kind of mission –'

'Same here,' and Murdo grinned his disarming grin.

'We're in the way of wanting to acquire some real estate in
the area, Sir, and we want to establish relationships with those
who own land hereabouts.'

Now it was the Minister's turn to feign surprise.

'You want to buy my Church?'

Mac glanced at Danny. Was there a delicate way of putting
this? Danny was no help. No, there wasn't.

'Well . . . not as a going concern.'

Two jet bombers screamed overhead as if engaged in some tremendous mating ritual. Two thuds from behind the cliffs and two columns of smoke rising into the blue indicated that consummation had taken place.

'They practise here,' said the Reverend Macpherson turning his two acquaintances away from the Church and walking them down the path towards the beach.

'The way I look at it is this; if they are bombing the beach, they cannot be bombing anywhere else. I take much comfort in that.'

From the Church windows the villagers strained to see what was taking place. Others had their ears to the door. Gordon was motioning to them to sit down and be still. Their curiosity could endanger the whole enterprise. But Murdo seemed to be doing splendidly.

'So far as your business here is concerned, gentlemen, all I can recommend is that you talk to our Mr Urquhart. He looks after the interests of the Church, *and* of the villagers.'

'We have spoken to him,' Danny interjected, but Macintyre overrode him.

'I understand. It sounds like excellent advice, Minister. Now I know that I scarcely have to mention this, but will you treat our conversation with confidence in the mean time?'

'I give you my word that I shall be as discreet as the next man, but news does tend to travel fast around here.'

As though giving visual emphasis to Murdo's remarks, the villagers began to sneak out of the Church, Gordon leading them. In ones and twos, in scurrying dribs and furtive drabs, they scuttled from the exposed outpost of the Church to the security of the village, while Mac and Danny continued on their downward path to the beach. At the point where scrub gave way to sand they spied the beachcomber picking his way along the shore. Glancing back at the Church Danny noticed with surprise the guilty stream of villagers, but Macintyre was busy feeling sorry for himself.

'I don't know what I'm doing here', he muttered. 'This is not me. I'm a Telex man. I could sew this whole thing up in one afternoon on the wires. You should have seen how I sorted out Mexico. Wham, bam, thank you, Macintyre. That's the kind of person I am. I need electricity.'

Another detachment of jets zoomed overhead. Macintyre seemed personally affronted. As soon as he could be heard he said to Danny:

'How about those jets? They really spoil a very nice area.'

Oldsen agreed. 'It's a crime,' he said.

Alone in his Church, the Reverend Murdo Macpherson was able to complete the prayer which Roddy had interrupted a few minutes earlier.

'Oh Lord, I bless and praise You for bringing to My Church today all these fine people. I know that You will guard and protect them in all that they do; also Lord that You will not forget the supplications of this Your most humble servant, for though I am but a weak and empty vessel, I have laboured in Your service.'

To prove the point Murdo at once set about putting his Church to rights. Gordon had distributed leaflets to the villagers as they entered the place, and these were now scattered throughout the Church. There was gum in the font and a mackerel head on the floor.

But Murdo was pleased. It gave him the opportunity to do some extra labouring in the Lord's service in the expectation of some extra beneficence from on high. He decided to go down on his hands and knees and pick up all the litter in his teeth. Short of cleaning the Church with his tongue there was little else he could undertake to prove his sincerity.

*

That night at dinner Mac asked Gordon Urquhart about the beachcomber. His name, it seemed, was Ben, and he lived in his shack all the year round. Didn't he feel the cold, Mac wondered, but Gordon assured him that Ben was quite used to anything the elements chose to hurl at him; indeed, the rougher the sea the better was he pleased, for he could expect to find a fine harvest of pickings after a violent storm. Should there be a wreck ... Mac was intrigued and tried to imagine what it would be like living in such conditions, and what sort of person would prefer it to, say, a penthouse in Houston – really weird.

His musings were interrupted by Gordon inquiring whether he had enjoyed his *lapin* casserole. The food had been particularly tasty that evening, and he was pleased to be able to say so. Gordon seemed pleased, for he left the dining-room smiling. But Danny was not smiling. A facility for languages is not always a blessing.

'*Lapin*,' he said, 'that's rabbit.'

When Gordon reappeared with a bottle of wine – compliments of the house – Mac asked him pointedly:

'Is this my rabbit?'

Gordon studied the bones on the plate with some care before agreeing that it was.

'Harry!' said Danny startled.

'Trudi!' said Mac stunned.

Gordon's face was grave as he explained: 'We don't allow animals in the bedrooms. I should have told you sooner. I'm sorry.'

'It was a pet, not an animal,' cried Mac. 'She had a name. You don't eat things with names. This is horrific!'

'It was an injured rabbit, that's all.' Gordon did not sound in the least repentant. 'It was in shock, with a broken limb, maybe more than one. It was in pain.'

Danny said: 'Excuse me, Mr Urquhart, but I think you were a bit hasty. Mac was looking after it. All it needed was lots of rest, and the proper treatment. There was every chance of a full recovery and a fully active life. Mac was on top of the situation.'

Hearing raised voices, Stella emerged from the kitchen. She was wearing an unusually tight sweater, which made Mac, already suffering a sense of loss, feel sentimental.

'They didn't like the rabbit,' Gordon said. But this was so obviously unfair that Danny burst out more passionately than before:

'Mac *loved* the rabbit – that's the point. It had a name. Two names actually!' So intense was Danny's passion that he was forced to his feet and dragged out of the room.

Using a fork to investigate the bones in the empty casserole dish, Gordon said: 'I'm sorry. I'm not sure if there's a lot I can do though. Is it worth calling the vet, Stella?'

Stella was not amused and snapped at her husband: 'Don't be a clown, Gordon. Get into the kitchen and make some coffee.'

The sharpness of her tone surprised Mac, who had never heard her speak roughly to anyone before. Was it possible that all was not as it seemed between this couple who had appeared to personify wedded bliss? Gordon obeyed her, but turned, as he was about to enter the kitchen, and remarked coolly as ever:

'It had a broken leg. A clean snap. You can check the bones in the dish if you don't believe me.'

As soon as Gordon had left the room, Stella sat down next to Mac and studied him intently.

'I'm sorry, Mac, but we eat rabbits here. The vet would have done the same. I didn't know it had a name.'

'It's OK, Stella.' The strange thing was that, although Mac felt genuinely cut up about the rabbit, he felt that he was receiving more sympathy from Stella than was appropriate. There were questions that remained unanswered. Stella was the cook. Had she recognized the rabbit? Had she even killed the rabbit? If Gordon had killed it, had Stella expostulated with him? If she had not complained to him then why did she seem so angry with him now? Gordon found it all quite baffling. Without thinking he speared more of the meat on his fork and raised it to his mouth.

'Look, you don't have to finish it, if you don't want to. How was it anyway?'

'It was nice. Apart from it being Trudi, it was nice.'

'What lovely long eyelashes you have,' said Stella softly. Mac thought he must have misheard.

'Was it a wine sauce?'

'Yeh. I just let it simmer for a couple of hours in some white wine. I'll let you have the recipe, if you like. Why did you call it Trudi?'

'No reason,' lied Mac, sucking on a bone.

Danny's room overlooked the sea. Much upset by the scene downstairs, he threw open the windows and leaned out. The Atlantic was nothing like the North Sea, beside which he had spent all his twenty-eight years. The Atlantic was generous, where the North Sea was mean. The Atlantic – or this part of it, at least – was warm, where the North Sea was bitter cold. Peculiar to the North East coast were such curious birds as the velvet scoter, the sanderling and the roseate terni; on the north-west coast the birds ran riot. The people too . . . In Fraserburgh they were hard-faced, jug-eared, calculating, little Aberdonians; in Ferness they were pleasure-loving (or seemed so), relaxed, inquisitive. As for the air . . . he gulped a generous lung-full of it, and found it warm, odiferous, gentle. Staring at the sea, as he often did on these long, light, lonely evenings, he sometimes fancied that he saw things. Shapes in the water, seals, sea-monsters . . . and Marina. Sitting on a rock (but this was *stupid*) and smiling at him. Not herself moving, and not enabling him to move, for if he left the window would she still be there when he reached the shore? If he had created her from his fevered imagination, he could create her again, but he felt certain that she was an independent creature. She had seemed so on the only occasion on which they had met, and he had no reason to suppose that she had changed. One thing was beyond doubt. She could not have come out of the North Sea.

He stayed at the window until long after Macintyre, who loved his clothes for a full ten minutes every night, had gone to sleep. He stayed staring at the sea until the waves sparkled and danced, and he could no longer be sure whether or not their glitter was real. He stayed so long that he could not be sure whether *anything* was real. At length, ravaged by lack of sleep, he stumbled to bed, and the coolness of the pillow was real enough – but only for a moment.

Everyone in Ferness was talking about money; everyone, that is, except Mac and Danny, and they were skimming stones into the sea. Iain saw money in terms of matchbox labels; he would be able to buy the Eberhaus collection, which was to come up at Sotheby's in a few weeks' time. Then he would have them all, every matchbox label in the world up until 1980.

'What will you do then, Iain?' asked Edward on the jetty. Iain considered.

'Go back to fishing,' he said.

Edward had no doubts. He would invest in a Rolls Royce, or, if he could lay his hands on one, a Bentley 3½-litre saloon by Park Ward.

'The '35?' Roddy asked.

'Mebbe. Apart from anything else a Rolls or a Bentley will last for ever. It's a false economy, to invest in cheap goods.'

'It's not cheap! The Maserati's over thirty thousand, and it looks nicer.'

The older man scoffed. 'I can just see you getting four or five winter lambs and a box of mackerel into the back of a Maserati. That's what you need your Rolls for, its space, its adaptability.'

Peter had decided to go into krugerrands. Gordon agreed

with him that in a strife-torn world gold and armaments were the only two commodities that could be depended upon. Gordon was also able to buy Peter krugerrands without the imposition of VAT.

'Aye, VAT's a sod,' Edward agreed.

Roddy said: 'Gordon recommends that I should buy myself a block of shares in one of the malt breweries, enough to get myself onto the Board. He says that people will always drink Scotch.'

These sentiments were echoed approvingly by some of the dour bystanders. Gideon also. Gideon was busily intent upon repainting the name of his boat; it was now to be called 'The Silver Dollar'. Alex, who was said to be over a hundred and thumped anyone who doubted it, watched Gideon intently.

'Are ye sure there are two L's in dollar, Gideon?'

'Yes,' said Gideon glowering, 'and there are two G's in bugger off!'

. In the office of the hotel Stella was doing the accounts while Gordon serviced the villagers' claim forms.

'He hasn't made a move yet?' Stella asked. In money matters she had the greatest respect for Gordon's acumen, although in other ways he was, of course, a big baby.

'I'll give him until tonight. I have to find out what kind of money he has to play with.'

'What do you reckon?'

'Millions,' said Gordon.

Stella looked at him sharply. 'How many?' she asked in a low voice.

'How about it, Stella? Shall we serve the rabbit soup tonight?'

'How many millions, Gordon?'

'Shit, I don't know. Mebbe five . . . ten . . . Hey, look at this. Would you believe Roddy's middle name?'

Stella did not press him further. If he knew, *when* he knew, he would tell her. What would she do with her share of the money? To begin with, she thought, she would like just to look at it. As she imagined piles of fives, tens, twenties and fifties (would they pay in dollars or pounds?) her period started.

'It's the wrist', said Mac, 'that's what the skill is. It's like a kind of flick – no – don't wave your arm about.'

Mac's suit looked incongruous on the beach and his crocodile shoes were stained with tar; Danny on the other hand looked immaculate. But he had a lot to learn about skimming pebbles.

'Look,' he cried, 'look, Mac, I got a six.'

'That's nothing, I got a ten earlier. You never saw it, but I did. I think ten is the maximum you can get before it sinks. It's a scientific fact, man.'

Danny: 'It's to do with the size too. A middle kind of size seems to work best. You'd never get ten out of a huge boulder.'

'Sure you could if you could get the velocity and angle of projection right. *Sure* you could.'

'The dam-busters did it with bouncing bombs,' said Danny, 'there was a film about it.'

The mention of bombs seemed to depress Mac, who dropped his handful of stones. Danny said that he wanted to check out the cliffs.

'I'll hang around the village for a while,' said Mac, 'and maybe catch Urquhart later. 'Hey,' he shouted after Danny, 'I said it! Urquhart!' And indeed, it sounded quite authentic, 'Urquhart! Urquhart!'

The gulls picked up the cry as Mac turned away from the sea and walked towards the village. Rikki was on the rampage with his motor-bike, but Mac was growing canny, and even waved as the helmeted tear-away roared past.

Skimming pebbles into the sea! How long was it since he had last done that? How long since he had walked on a beach? How long, for Christ's sake, since he had walked anywhere that wasn't from a car to a car? These people! They handled things. They pulled fish from the sea and brushed paint onto walls and hunted for driftwood and mended engines. He knew nobody in Houston – except Lester – who handled things. They dealt in *names* of things and *numbers* of things, and *prices* of things, and *demand* for things, but what did they know of the *things* themselves, the feel of them? He had reached the jetty where a group of fishermen were working on their creels, picturesquely grouped as though for a tourist film. Mac felt a surge of benevolence towards them. He wished he was dressed like them in a sweater or a windcheater, in Wellington boots and a small woollen hat.

'Working hard?' he inquired with a genial twist of the head.

'Aye,' they said.

'What are you doing there?'

'Fixing the creels,' they said and Roddy added: 'Trying to keep the lobsters in and the crabs out.'

Automatically Mac's mind reverted to a restaurant on Highway 16, and a fish-tank, and Trudi, naked in it, and him walking round it, only when Trudi came face to face with him through the glass sides of the tank, it was not Trudi's face, but Stella's with her curly hair and her sulky mouth which promised so much.

'What do you do with the lobsters?'

Roddy glanced around the group, eyes twinkling, but Peter gave the merest shake of his head, so Roddy contented himself with saying:

'They catch an aeroplane every night at Inverness – next day they're being eaten in London or Paris. They see the world!'

'Don't you eat them?'

'Oh no, too expensive.' Mac recognized Roddy as the man who had organized the 10p's for him at the bar of the Macaskill Arms.

'You work here as well as the bar?'

'Aye, we all muck in together. Do any job that needs doing. Don't we, lads?' The lads agreed that they did.

'Have you only got *one* job?' Peter inquired in surprise.

'Only one.' Mac bowed his head to study his shuffling feet. These were good people. He hoped they thought well of him, although he only had the one job. Iain asked,

'Telephone-box all right?'

'Sure, sure.'

'Gideon's going to paint it up for you. Any colour you fancy?' Hearing his name Gideon turned from his boat. The pot of red paint dangled under Mac's nose.

'Red,' he said. 'Red's fine.'

There was general agreement that Mac had made a wise decision. No doubt about it – red was quite the best colour for a telephone-box. But Mac had a suggestion to make. The locals on the jetty waited anxiously to hear it. He said:

'The cord could be a bit longer.' Cord?

'Wire,' Roddy interpreted. Iain nodded his head. The wire *was* short.

'In America,' Mac continued, 'the cord tends to be a bit longer.' Helpfully he made a gesture to indicate 'longer'. The locals looked at his gesturing hands with interest. Longer cords in America; whatever next?

Wretched at being ignored for so long in a world of its own creation, a baby in a push-chair started bawling.

'Whose baby is that?' Mac inquired pleasantly. It was not a question anyone on the Ferness jetty was prepared to answer.

Embarrassment polluted the air. Mac wished himself safely back in his penthouse or in his office in Happer Tower. Himself, he was a Telex man.

The sun was warm. The sea sparkled like frosted glass. Who could tell what it contained? Danny Oldsen skipped across the rocks studded with limpets, sure-footed in his brogues. He no longer disliked Mac, but preferred to be by himself. The sea breeze caressed his face. On a skerry perched a pair of shags, dark brown and dissatisfied-looking, while the surf teased their tail feathers. Drifting a few hundred yards offshore and unobserved by Danny was a creel boat, in whose wheel-house the skipper stood and focused his binoculars. After watching Danny's progress for a few minutes, the skipper, a stocky man who looked capable of wrestling a blue whale into submission, picked up the microphone of his CB radio and started to transmit –

'Captain Bluebeard to General Stores . . . Captain Bluebeard to General Stores . . . do it to me, Good Lady . . .'

The Good Lady whom Captain Bluebeard was trying to contact was indeed at the General Stores; she was Mrs Fraser who ran it. There she sold everything except dreams and perhaps, if you had insisted, she might have found an old packet of them tucked away between the battledores and the butter-muslin. It was a post office, a chemist's, a clothing store, a hardware shop, a fancy goods emporium, a library, a stationer's, a grocer's and a supplier of electrical equipment.

Mac had gone there to buy some toothpaste and shampoo. Mrs Fraser, who reminded him of his mother, had asked did he want dry, normal or greasy, and Mac, as though his virility was being impugned, said:

'Normal. Extra normal.'

'Normal,' Mrs Fraser had said, fetching it down from between the buckwheat and the Wellington boots, 'and does dandruff too.' It was then that her CB radio had crackled into life and the skipper's voice rang out:

'Bluebeard to General Store . . . come on, Good Lady . . . Bluebeard on Channel . . . come on . . .' Mrs Fraser was equal to the situation. She excused herself gracefully and trotted to the back room where she took the microphone from the wall. She spoke quietly into it, quietly, but with menace.

SPOILING A VERY NICE AREA

'General Store to Bluebeard . . . you're breaking the windows Bluebeard.' But Bluebeard was so full of his news that he was not to be silenced.

'You're breaking the needles also, Good Lady. I have an eye-ball on the junior business suit. He's on the rocks. Could be a couple of hours. Come back sweet thing?' Mrs Fraser's voice was steely now as she explained: 'I'm jaw-jacking with Uncle Sam this time . . . will you listen out, Bluebeard.' And to her relief came the reply:

'I've copied the mail, Good Lady. Bluebeard out and final.' Improvising courageously, Mrs Fraser shouted to the now dead air waves: 'That'll be two pints of milk and two pounds of sugar – right you are!' Then smiling again that sweet maternal smile, because the poor lad was a long way from his home, Mrs Fraser returned to the front room of the general stores to see if she could sell Mac a pair of swimming flippers or a rechargeable pocket calculator with thirty-eight functions to add to his fluoride toothpaste and extra-normal hair shampoo. She could not, but he did ask for ten pounds worth of 10p pieces, since he knew he was going to need to make several telephone calls.

There was no reason on earth, there was no reason in the sea, why she should have been there. But Danny fancied that if he wanted her urgently enough, why there she would be. He wanted her there very urgently and, some twenty feet below where he stood on the cliffs, there she was. She had come walking out of the sea. He had not known it was her. He had not known *what* it was, for she, Marina, had been wearing a wet-suit and a face-mask with an air-tank on her back. She had removed the tank and the mask and shaken her hair loose (as a labrador shakes itself upon emerging from the water), and, of course, then he had known. He had laid down among the rocks, among the heather and the machair, and spied on her.

But she knew. Although she had her back to him, she knew. She turned towards him.

'Come down!' she called, and then more sternly, because he had sunk lower into the landscape when she called: 'Come here! I want to talk to you!' By the time he reached her she was washing specimens in a rock pool.

'Sting winkle,' she said.

'Sorry?'

'*Ocenebra erinacea*, otherwise known as a drill. Looks harmless doesn't it? But it isn't, not to another mollusc. It feeds on them by boring through their shells.'

'Really?'

'You're Mr What's-his-name from Knox.' It wasn't a question. Danny held out his hand and introduced himself.

'We met in Aberdeen,' he added.

'I remember.' She had a brisk way of speaking, that made everything she said sound pertinent and authoritative; yet she looked very young. Scarcely more than a child, thought Danny. Now that he was close to her there was no mistaking the fishy odour.

In an attempt to make polite conversation, Danny asked: 'Did you swim all the way?'

'No. I stay here a lot. This is *my* bay.' She glanced around her proprietorially. 'I'm working on a biological profile of the whole place. Didn't Geddes tell you?'

'Not in so many words.'

'I'm plotting everything, salinity, seaweed, ornithology, plankton and krill, molluscs and bivalves, cyclostomes, currents, everything from the two headlands right inshore to the high-tide mark.'

'How's the water? Cold?'

'Not as cold as it should be. We're right in the path of the North Atlantic Drift here – the Gulf Stream, warmish water from the Caribbean – which is what makes it so special. You see, where it meets the cold water from the Arctic it produces great turbulence, which brings all the richest nutrients up from the deep – hence all these marine organisms and the fish, birds, seals and whales which feed on them.'

'There's nothing like that in Fraserburgh,' said Danny, impressed.

'You'd be surprised. Do you swim?'

'Not from Fraserburgh. Not that far.'

'How are things in the village?'

'OK.'

For the first time Marina looked at him sharply and paused for a moment before saying: 'They're good people. Let me know if I can help.'

'The winkle . . . is it sleeping?'

'Och no, it's dead. Take it if you like. You can eat them you know.' Danny smiled and shook his head: 'Though it would make a change from rabbit,' he muttered.

On his way back from the stores and looking forward to cleaning his normal teeth and shampooing his normal hair, Mac was arrested by the sound of sultry music from the hotel dining-room. It was significantly louder and a good deal more agreeable than the Musack which was played at meal-times, and it was accompanied by shuffling noises and giggling. The door was ajar. Mac craned his head to see around it.

The tables were partially laid for dinner, but the lights were off. Gordon and Stella were dancing. Gordon was wearing his apron and had a dish-cloth thrown casually over his shoulder. A coffee cup dangled from the little finger of Stella's left hand which was draped around Gordon's neck. They were holding each other tightly. While Mac watched, Gordon, with a fancy piece of footwork learned from who knows what Hollywood musical, twisted Stella around in his arms and bent her over backwards, so that he was leaning over her, their mouths very close, their breath mingling; they didn't kiss. Gordon was smiling, but in Stella's eyes there was an expression of wistfulness, the look of a person straining to recall the precise quality of past happiness – or so it seemed to Mac. They danced on, weaving between the tables. Mac could bear to watch no longer, but no more could he bear to return to his solitary room. He left his toothpaste and shampoo on the hall table and returned to the jetty, where his friends were.

'Do you have any idea how many crustaceans there are in the world?' Marina was holding a baby crab by the shell and studying it intently. 'The blue whale, the largest animal in the world, and the tiniest transparent fishes, so small that you could easily hold a hundred in your hand, both depend upon crustaceans for their food supply. And they don't only live in water: a vast multitude of them are parasites living on you, Danny, and on me.'

'Do you know why we're here?'

'The human race in general, or you and Mr Macintyre in particular?'

'Me and Mac.'

'Of course. Everyone knows. They've been smelling the money ever since you two arrived.' She smiled. 'They must be going crazy.'

'And you don't mind?'

'Why should I mind? It's my project, isn't it?'

Danny was perplexed by this. '*Your* project?'

'Sure. The Marine Laboratory, right? I sent the proposals to Houston months ago, and you're here to check it out. Don't be coy.' Rather than being coy, Danny played for time. 'Sure . . . The Marine Laboratory.'

'Oh, don't worry. I know it's only a public relations number for Knox right now, but the sea is where the future is, not the stars.' She added simply: 'It's where we came from, you see, where we belong.'

'I'm afraid I'm not a great swimmer myself.'

Marina strapped on her air-tank, and zipped her wet-suit up to her neck. Holding the face-mask, she stepped into the sea.

'Of course you are,' she said. 'All you do is do it. But I have to go now.' She walked into the water until it reached her breasts, then turned to smile.

'When can I see you?' Danny asked, reluctant to let her go.

'I'm always around. I'll pop up and see you again soon.'

'You got enough air to get home?'

'Yes. Sure.'

'Take care anyway.'

'See you.' As she tucked her hair under her face-mask she was directly in line with the setting sun. Danny could not look at her.

'Have you got a telephone number or anything?' he cried, but the surface of the sea was unbroken and all that remained to remind him that the encounter had not been a dream was the widening circle of ripples in the sea, and a sense of something precious which he had once seen and might never recapture. Soon even the ripples had gone.

It was Fraser, the local intellectual and consequently the one whose finances were the most precarious, who led the deputation to the Macaskill Arms that evening. Fraser, from whom the thickest skinned of London publishers flinched when he made his sporadic raids on London, demanding to see such confidential things as royalty statements and publishers' accounts, had no fear of Texan oilmen or hotel-keepers, and told Gordon as much. He quoted Scott at him:

' "Jock, when ye hae nothing else to do, ye may be ay sticking in a tree; it will be growing, Jock, when ye're sleeping",' and made such a noise that Gordon was forced to buy him a whisky on the house to shut him up long enough to put his own arguments. ('You shouldn't encourage him, Gordon,' said Mrs

75

Fraser, who didn't.) The burden of Fraser's complaint – and he seemed to have the support of most of the village – was that the thing to do was simply to get Macintyre to make an offer. What harm was there in an offer? One was not obliged to accept it.

'It's not that simple,' said Gordon. 'We can't appear too eager. We string him along, and the price goes up; don't you see that?'

'But what if he pulls out?' Mrs Fraser asked. Being married to an intellectual was just as bad as being one, intellectuals being notoriously difficult to get out of bed in the morning, and fond of their food.

'It's too much of a gamble,' said Fraser. 'We think you should ask him what he has to offer right now.' There were murmurs of assent from those who had not been bought whiskies on the house. Gordon looked at them much as his namesake had looked at the rabble at Khartoum.

'I told you I needed your trust and your patience. Let me take the strain for a day or so. Relax. Give me until the ceilidh, just another twenty-four hours.'

Whether or not they would have accepted Gordon's terms will never be known, for at that moment Macintyre, who was increasingly feeling himself a part of the village, although it was a feeling which the village did not reciprocate, entered the pub, his pockets clinking with 10p pieces.

'OK, we'll talk at the ceilidh,' Fraser muttered as Gordon refilled his tumbler.

'Nice to see you in here, Mr Macintyre.'

'Mr Urquhart,' said Mac. He enjoyed saying the name now that he knew how it was done and savoured it on his tongue.

Gordon reached into the recesses of the bar where, concealed behind a hardboard partition cut in Moorish shapes vaguely reminiscent of the Alhambra, he kept a rather precious bottle. It was covered in dust and its label was stained and faded, but it was more than two thirds full of golden liquid, and that was what mattered. Fraser's intellectual eyes followed it like Eliot following Pound.

'The Macaskill, a pure malt whisky,' said Gordon with pride. 'Forty-two years old.' There was a respectful silence in the bar, broken rather too soon when Mac said:

'Old enough to be out on its own,' and smirked. Even Gordon was hard put to it to manage a smile at this. But barmen, he knew, must always flatter their customers, especially when these customers are oilmen from Texas, so:

'Very true,' he said, and added, pouring a second glass, 'Slange!'

'Yeh,' Mac agreed.

Encouraged by the whisky, which tasted like the juice of the sun, Gordon suggested that they leave the bar for a private talk, and Roddy took his place. Fraser chuckled. Not only had Gordon learned sense, it seemed, but he had left – whether by accident or design – the Macaskill on the bar, and Roddy was an easy touch.

Gordon knew what he was doing when he gave Mac a dram of Macaskill and took him onto the beach in the twilight of high summer. In the gloaming men and women say and do things which at other times and in other places they would never consider. The sky is scarlet, the sea is dark, the swell is heavy and the rocks stand out in black profile. Gordon was used to it, could allow for it, but for Mac the gloaming was uncanny and alarming. Together they roamed in it and talked about money, while the beach listened. Even the gulls were muted.

'It's not just a matter of fixing a price,' began Gordon, 'There are emotions to be considered. People get attached to a place like this.'

'I can appreciate that,' said Mac. He could.

'I have to be able to offer them more than just money . . .'

'How about *more* money?'

'It's not just a matter of buying off people's feelings – it's not as crude as that – it's more a matter of taking their feelings, well, into account.'

'I don't disagree.'

'We're talking about massive disturbance, the end of an old-established way of life, resettlement, people picking up the pieces and starting again.'

'Sounds like a lot of money,' said Mac doubtfully, 'the way you put it.'

'One way it strikes me might be a trust fund over and above the purchase price, a way of letting the community feel involved in the place, say a lump sum plus a percentage of profits over ten or twenty years. With some local trustees and some from Knox.'

'We have to settle on a basic price first. Then I'll know how I can accommodate the frills.'

'OK,' said Gordon, 'I'll get you a fixed price averaging over the whole area.'

'Good.'

There was the sound of a universal sigh, as a flock of birds flapped into the air and wheeled overhead with cries of 'klee-eep' 'klee-eep'. Their pied bodies flickered in what was left of the daylight and their orange beaks looked black against the sky.

'What are these birds?'

'Oyster-catchers. They come with the beach.'

But still Mac said nothing about the sums of money he had to spend, so cautiously Gordon suggested:

'We have to be talking about millions . . .'

'Maybe . . .' said Mac cheerfully enough, but he still wished it could have been done by telex.

'What kind of millions do you reckon we're talking about?'

'Oh, we'll have to talk about that.'

'So, let's talk about it,' said Gordon. There was another pause. Growing bored, the oyster-catchers had moved north along the coast, singing a brief hymn as they passed the Church. 'I was thinking of maybe a target figure of ... twenty million?'

'For the trust?'

'For the community, yes. Pounds.'

'Dollars maybe,' said Mac sadly. It was not going to be difficult after all. Soon his business would be concluded. What was it that Stella had said about his eyelashes?

'It's a nice evening though,' said Gordon Urquhart relieved. He had named his price, which was as high as he had dared to go and, while not accepting it, Mac had not flinched. Negotiations could proceed apace – Mac agreed that it was indeed a nice evening.

For Danny Oldsen it was a frustrating evening. He had returned after dinner to the spot from which he had last seen Marina; he would have wished to be nowhere else. He was convinced that when she next came to visit him – and she would – she would come from the sea, which was how we all evolved. She moves in a mysterious way her wonders to perform, he thought, adding to himself that she probably also planted her footsteps on the sea and rode upon the storm. Anyway, whether or not she would come again to visit him so soon after her previous visit, he must be there to welcome her. Literature was littered with examples of men who, had they waited just a very little longer, would have been rewarded with the Princess, but who lacked faith. *He* wouldn't lack faith. *He* would wait for as long as was needful and, while he waited, he would endeavour not to leap so excitedly to his feet every time a fish jumped, or a cormorant pierced the sea with its rough beak.

Gordon, as well as Mac, felt a good deal more relaxed now that a sum of money had been mentioned. Mac was a more experienced negotiator, although most of his skill had been learnt over the wires, but Gordon, as hotelier, as cab-driver, as investment adviser, knew almost all that was worth knowing about human nature. Put up an electronic whizz-kid against a behavioural psychologist and you will have a close contest, electronics being irresistible and psychology immovable. Mac had taken a slight advantage by forcing Gordon to name a figure, but Gordon, by refusing to specify that he was dealing in pounds when Mac would have assumed dollars, had parried cleverly. Now the real bargaining could begin, and the two men, seeing that Ben had a good fire going in front of his shack, repaired thither.

Ben's face had been lined by the wind and cracked by the frost and pitted by the sand. His eyes were shrewd and he seemed to apply the same standards to people as to jetsam; he could afford to pick and choose. He had his hands around a mug of tea, and the firelight dappled his face.

'Evening Ben,' said Gordon Urquhart.

As a child Gordon had been taken into Ben's shack and shown the mysteries of the Orient: a rug from a nomadic tribe in China; an ivory bauble in which were contained seven smaller ivory baubles. The whole thing carved mysteriously from a single piece of ivory; a row of immortals glazed in a china so white that it made the eyes dazzle to look at them. But then he grew up. Such treasures were not for adult eyes, he knew that, but still he felt betrayed by the cheerful old man.

'It's a pleasant night, Gordon.'

'This is Macintyre, Ben. He's staying with us for a time.' Ben glanced at the American. 'I'd offer you some tea but there's only the one other cup.'

Gordon said: 'We don't mind sharing.' As a child he had received the strangest of sweets from Ben, Turkish Delight, chocolate cigars, and curiously spicy ones that tasted of gin; one never knew what to expect. Surely Ben would not now begrudge him a cup of tea. Mac said that he would not mind sharing either, so long as the tea was unsugared, and at his request Ben stamped off to fetch the other cup. The firelight on the faces, the formality in the men's behaviour, the actual way in which the cup went back and forth, gave the occasion a ceremonial, almost a mystical quality. With a hint of mischief, Gordon said:

'Macintyre was asking me how much I thought the bay was worth, Ben.'

Ben chuckled. His chuckles, as he looked first at the hotel-keeper, then at the solemn American, became hearty, became a bellow of laughter. Still laughing: 'That's a good one, Gordon,' he said. 'What was it you wanted to fix a price on? Was it the sand, or the water, or just everything?'

'Just everything,' said Mac.

Ben's laughter continued, became universal, laughter at the folly of mankind rather than merely at these two foolish men. In the village they could just hear the laughter, and they smiled. In his Church, Murdo, hearing it, put down his battered Raymond Chandler paperback for a moment and lit a cigar. On his rock Danny Oldsen heard it, and thought it was mocking *him*, and covered his ears. At last Ben's laughter stopped, possibly because he could not drink his tea while laughing. The sky had darkened now and was freckled with stars.

'Do you know about the stars, Ben?' Mac asked.

'I know my way around *this* sky.'

'What about comets? Are there any around?'

Ben smiled. 'Do you want to buy a comet as well?'

'Maybe,' said the cautious Macintyre.

'If you want to find a comet all you have to do is look long enough – in the right place.'

'Where would you look?'

'If I had the inclination I would look in Leo, but it seems like an awful lot of trouble just to find a comet. They're of no use, you know. They have no gravitational pull, and the chance of one hitting us today is about two hundred million to one.'

'Us?' Gordon asked. Ben spread his arms wide to indicate a universal us.

'What about Virgo?'

Before Ben could reply, Gordon, with a characteristically serious face, said: 'You didn't mention comets before, Macintyre. You're opening up a whole new area of negotiation.'

Mac looked sharply at him. Was the guy serious? Mac smiled. Gordon smiled. Ben poured himself another cup of tea. Gordon rose to his feet.

'We'll leave you in peace now, Ben. Listen, we're having a ceilidh tomorrow, after Mac and I have tidied up some work. You'll come?'

'I'll be there, Gordon, you can count on that.'

Macintyre had just put down his cup of tea, when he saw something so startling that he could not believe it. All around him the velvet of the sky was streaked with flashes of white light. It was as though a thousand huge matches had all flared at once and were being thrust down to be snuffed in the sea.

'Jesus, look!' he cried. Then, as the flashes continued: 'Holy Christ!' And then, as he wondered whether the two hundred million to one shot had happened and a comet was about to strike them: 'Jesus!'

'Calm down, Mac,' said Urquhart, but even his voice was a little tremulous, 'it's just a meteor shower.'

The tide had come in around the rock on which Danny waited. The meteor shower was reflected in the waves, so that he seemed to be at the centre of it all. He remembered a picture he had seen of Saint Sebastian, was it, stuck full of arrows. He was the saint and the arrows were arrows of light. He was transfixed. Was it Marina's work? Was the show just for him? He could believe it. He could believe anything of her. He wanted to.

When the last meteorite had completed its elliptical orbit and drowned itself somewhere in the Atlantic, Danny hauled himself back to the hotel. His clothes were damp and his lips salt with spray, but he was reluctant to undress, and wherever his skin touched the Rayon of his pyjamas, or the cotton of his sheets, it puckered. Was dryness natural, he wondered, to humans, who started their evolutionary process in the sea and their life-cycle in the amniotic fluid of the womb. Certainly the idea of being buried in the ground or consumed to ashes was repellent to him now. He dreamed fishy, scaly dreams that were not altogether pleasant, and awoke with the clearest recollection of the events of the past evening. He ran a bath. With the water just a degree or two warmer than the temperature of his body, Danny allowed himself to sway with it. His toe-nails were like white tortoiseshell limpets (*Acmeae virginea*), his genitals like a crab concealed in seaweed, his body vast and unnecessary. He set the stopwatch on his digital watch and ducked his head under water. When he emerged he discovered that he had held his breath for a mere forty seconds. One couldn't travel far in forty seconds! He practised, filling his lungs and releasing the air as slowly as possible, until he was able to stay submerged for more than a minute. It was a start, something to build on.

Macintyre was surprised when Danny hurried his breakfast. It was not typical of the man, and Mac felt rushed by Danny's impatience. Once Danny attempted to engage Mac in conversation.

'Did you know,' he said, 'that under water everything looks twenty-five per cent bigger?'

'Sure I knew that. That's why skinny-dipping was so popular when I was in fourth grade.'

Danny could make no sense of this at all. However, he did observe, with some curiosity, that Mac was not wearing a tie and that he had left off the jacket of his suit. As soon as he had

83

eaten the last morsel of smoked haddock, Danny, whose heightened sensitivity did not reduce his appetite, suggested a stroll to the jetty, but a stroll seemed the last thing on his mind when he felt the morning breeze on his cheek, for he was off like an untrained greyhound, past the jetty and halfway to the beach while Mac was still sniffing the air.

Rikki roared by, and the fumes from his Harley Davidson hung like bonfire smoke in the air against the white-washed cottages. Andrew tap-tapped away cheerfully at tiles on the hotel roof – there was nothing wrong with them until he got to work and Gideon flip-flopped his paintbrush on the telephone-kiosk. The revs of the engine, the taps of the hammer, the percussion of the brush and the disorderly squealing of the gulls creaked a concatenation of sound, as though Ferness were tuning itself up for the daily symphony. Until the ringing of the telephone ruined everything . . .

Paintbrush in hand, Gideon answered it, then trotted across the road to Mac.

'Mr Macintyre! Telephone! A Mr Houston!' This time Macintyre was relieved of the need to feed 10p's into the coin-box and would have been entirely relaxed as he passed the time of day (or night in Houston) with Happer, had it not been for Gideon leering at him through the glass.

'This is Happer. How are things, Macintyre?'

'Sir, they're fine. The deal is about there.'

'What about the sky?'

'The sky, Sir, is amazing. There seems to be a lot happening in it, all the time. Last night it was a meteor shower – that was spectacular.'

'Where was the shower, Macintyre?'

The question took him unawares. 'In the sky. They, well, came down.'

'Which part of the sky?'

'I don't know exactly Sir, but I've been told that comet-wise

Leo might be worth a look. Should I switch from Virgo, Sir? I'll have more time when we finalize the deal.'

'No, no. Do both, Macintyre. Leo and Virgo.'

'You ever seen a meteor shower, Sir?'

'I was there. Kitt Peak, Arizona, on the night of the 17th of November, 1966. Quite a night, Macintyre. One hundred and fifty thousand meteors per hour were recorded.'

'Take a lot of counting, Mr Happer?'

'Certainly did, son, certainly did. A sight worth seeing – I know how you must feel.'

'Thank you, Sir.'

'I'll keep in touch.'

'Good-bye, Sir, good-bye.'

7

HOUSTON

You can't make an omelette without breaking eggs

Moving from the telephone in his office to his private apartments took Happer past some of his most prized possessions. Here was Desaguliers Cometarium, a beautiful contraption made from cog-wheels and rotating rods. And here was an English Tellurion. By turning an ivory crank the movements of the earth in relation to the sun could be observed. But perhaps most beautiful of all was the large armillary sphere of Santucci della Pomarance, made in Italy in the sixteenth century and standing on carved and gilded feet in the shape of mermaids. Their bosoms were bare, they had mouths like fishes and they carried the solar system on their heads. But Happer was hungry.

He melted butter in the pan – it had to be heated until blue smoke, like the smoke from the exhaust of a Harley Davidson, began to rise. Then the beaten and seasoned eggs could be softly poured in. Thereafter it was merely a matter of jiggling the pan until the egg mixture was thin and *almost* set, at which point – the telephone rang. Goddammit. Happer took the call on the kitchen extension.

'Yes?' It was Moritz's voice:

'Happer?'

'Yes.'

'You're a shit, Happer, a useless piece of crap. Have I told you that already today?' From where he stood Happer could see the omelette solidifying into a lumpish pancake; the fat was beginning to burn. He could not quite reach the pan from the telephone.

'Get off the phone, Moritz. I don't need you any more. You're not getting paid. I'm a busy man. Leave me alone.'

'It worked again, Mr Happer. This is doing more good than the formal sessions, don't you agree?'

'There are no more sessions, so leave me alone, Moritz. I shall call the police. This is harassment.'

'Asshole, Crapper! You love it. Turd! Don't you? Craphound!' Happer replaced the receiver and moved fast to salvage whatever he could of his omelette. The cast-iron handle of the pan was so hot that, as he closed his fingers around it, they adhered to the metal. Happer shrieked and pulled his hand away. The pan and its contents smashed to the ground. The omelette split itself into a meteor shower of egg particles. Happer sat heavily down on a stool. After a while he felt that he was not alone in his private apartment. Tentatively he picked up the telephone receiver and put it to his ear. An all-too-familiar voice murmured silkily:

'I'm still here, Happer, and you're still a useless mother-f-.' Close to weeping with frustration, Happer slammed down the phone, a wrecked executive amidst the wreckage of his supper.

8

FERNESS

The truth about mermaids

It was low tide and the grey seals had come ashore. There was a cove to the leeside of the headland which they had made their own and hither, when the day was calm and sunny, they would come to lie basking on the rocks, their heads towards the sea, ready to dive off the rock-shelf as soon as they scented danger. Silvery grey or dusky or yellowish-white (the cubs) they would balance on their bellies, while the gentle Atlantic swell rolled them around. They grunted. Their eyes were half-closed, their contentment so complete that they could not bear, it seemed, to enjoy it in silence.

Marina had brought Danny to the seal-cove. When she emerged from the sea, he was already waiting on the rocks. He was convinced that if he were waiting, she would come. So he waited and she came and with proprietary pride took him off to see the seals. Danny said that they appeared 'nice and friendly'.

'They have teeth and claws,' said Marina, 'and are carnivorous.'

'Are they tame?'

'They wouldn't let you so close without me. A salmon fisherman would shoot them on sight. They steal his fish and ruin his nets and they know what they're doing. The greys are not docile like other seals, and some believe that they are less intelligent, but I know them well and they're rascals. We have to keep an eye on them though; there's only fifty thousand left in the Atlantic now.'

'Sailors used to think they were mermaids, didn't they?'

'Yes,' said Marina with a secret smile, 'but they were wrong.'

Meanwhile Mac had been investigating a rock-pool. It was deceptively clear so that when he reached in to take out a shell, he found that his whole arm was in the water before he had grabbed his prize. He had already removed his shoes and his watch, and now had squatted over his pool with all the intensity of a child. A small pile of choice items lay on the rock beside him.

Out in the bay a large trawler anchored. The Captain had picked up the news on his short-wave radio that a ceilidh was planned and Viktor Pinochkin was never one to miss a party. When he climbed into his launch he was observed by the coast-guard who passed the news to Bluebeard who passed it on to Mrs Fraser. The air-waves were humming and so was Mrs Fraser as she emerged excitedly from the general stores.

'Roddy!' she shouted across the street, 'tell Gordon Urquhart – the Russians are coming, the Russians are coming!'

It was an exaggeration. Only Viktor was coming. His launch was navigated into the harbour by a blonde Russian lady who was being rather more emotional than was advisable in a small boat. What was she complaining about so volubly? The watchers on the jetty could only speculate. From Archangel to Stornaway, and from Grimsby to Hamburg it was well known that it was no use getting possessive with Pinochkin. It was like trying to put handcuffs on the Niagara Falls.

Alerted by Roddy, Gordon Urquhart was there on the jetty to help the Russian ashore, which meant relieving him of a number of parcels which clinked, and receiving in return several slobbery bear-hugs.

'Good to see you, Viktor,' said Gordon.

'And good to see you too, but watch the booze. Silly beetch!' This last was shouted in the general direction of the blonde in the launch, who was still hurling cossack imprecations at Viktor, though the space between them was now unbridgeable, even by a cossack.

'The plum brandy is for Stella. The rest is the usual. How are things?'

'There is to be a ceilidh.'

'That I know.'

'Do you know that we have been invaded by America?' Gordon and Viktor were making for the hotel. 'Yes, we are all going to be rich. Really. We won't have anywhere to call home, but we'll be stinking rich.'

'Are the Americans here already? I do not think so. I see no hamburger joint. I hear no Doris Day. Where is the CIA?'

'So far we have just one American. And a Scots kid. They'll be somewhere on the beach. They have taken to going for long walks.'

'No, Gordon, he cannot be an American. They walk in beach buggies, in golf-carts, on trolley-cars with Miss Judy Garland.'

'Viktor, you are so out of date. When did you last see a film?' In a terrible imitation of Clark Gable, Victor said: 'Frankly, Gordon, I don't give a damn.'

The incoming tide had washed the seals off the rocks, and Danny had led Marina to his favourite spot on the cliffs whence on a clear day you could see the Outer Hebrides and where the grass was long and comforting. Marina had removed her head-mask and her slippers. Her golden hair was waist-long and despite everything appeared always to have been recently combed. She lay on her back in the grass, luxuriating in the warmth of the late morning sunshine, her head next to Danny's feet, her feet close by his head. His silliness comforted her. Although it was clear that he was already head over heels in love, he posed no kind of a threat to her peace of mind. All he proposed to do was teach her Japanese.

'Otoko,' he said and pointed to himself, 'me . . . Otoko.'

'Otoko,' said Marina, enjoying the sound.

'You . . . onna.'

'Onna . . . me.'

'Ooooona,' murmured Danny, pursing his lips and frowning, 'ooooona.'

'Ooooona . . . otoko.' And she closed her eyes for a moment to feel the sun on her eyelids. Danny stretched one arm out to the sea.

'Paiyoo. . . .' He pointed to Marina and did the breast-stroke in the air. 'Marina . . . paiyoo . . . sakana . . . asika . . . azarisi.' Marina no longer cared what the words meant. They were too beautiful to mean anything. She repeated: 'Me . . . sakana . . . asika . . . azarisi.' Danny looked long and passionately at Marina's left leg, encased as it was in a rubber sheath. He stroked it. He pointed to the knee.

'Asi . . . asi,' he said. She seemed content. She seemed pleased. She seemed not to mind. He kissed the knee and said:

'Kisu.' When he spoke Japanese he narrowed his eyes somewhat. He would have made a handsome samurai warrior.

Faking incomprehension, Marina asked: 'Ki-Su?'

Danny needed no further encouragement and gave the knee a second kiss.

Continuing the lesson, he explained: 'Kisu . . . kisu . . . seppum.' At which he moved his lips down the leg until he reached the bare skin of the ankle. Now his lips lingered with each kiss.

'You taste salty,' he said. She did. And fishy. The tiny hairs on her ankle were rough against his tongue. He licked his lips. Marina raised her head to look at him and said:

'You're on the fresh side.'

But if this was a warning to him to slow down, Danny refused to heed it. He held her left foot delicately in both his hands, as though it were a brandy glass with a peony floating in it. He kissed the ankle again, then the instep. When he reached the toes, he kissed each one with grave decorum, then delicately parted them one by one to press kisses in between them. But it was then that he noticed something which astonished and excited him more than anything had astonished, more than anything had excited him ever before, in Fraserburgh or Ferness, in a dream or awake. There was fine skin between her spreading toes. She had webbed feet. The sun shone through the webbing which was without bones or veins; it was just skin.

'Sakana?' Marina asked in her deep and humorous voice. 'Azarasi?' Danny shook his head as though to clear it. 'Ningyo,' he said.

'Ningyo . . . ningyo . . .' said Marina.

Of all the words she had learned that morning the Japanese word for mermaid was the most beautiful. She lay back on the grass and gazed into the sky. It was like looking down into the clearest of rock-pools. The clouds were sea-anemones. She hummed to herself a song she had always known.

At the foot of the cliff Mac's watch, abandoned on a rock, was being submerged by the sea. With what seemed like desperation it played over and over the first four bars of 'The Yellow Rose of Texas'. Its tiny cadmium heart would keep it alive and singing under the waves for weeks and weeks. Maybe the seals would enjoy it; or maybe Marina would.

*

The bar of the Macaskill Arms closed and the interior was gloomy and stale with last night's beer and last year's tobacco ash. But Gordon and Viktor noticed nothing of its squalor, or, if they did, cared less. They were discussing Viktor's investments. For rather less than the stock-exchange commission rate, Gordon handled all Viktor's finances, and was two thirds of the way to making him a very rich man. As Viktor signed the various documents which Gordon laid in front of him, Gordon took him through the details.

'I've left all of last year's money on short-term deposit. It didn't seem worthwhile moving it into stock and I didn't know when you might need it.'

'Wouldn't it work harder on the exchange?' Viktor asked wistfully. He hankered after share certificates.

'The amounts don't justify it, Viktor. If we're talking about half a million ... Besides, the dollar is all over the place just now. It would be a full time job monitoring it—or am I getting lazy?'

'You? Never. But I see what you mean.'

'You should think again about some property. That's the place to be when interest rates fall. Or I could get you some krugerrands free of VAT? I shall be pretty liquid myself once this Knox thing goes through – you could come in with me.'

'You know I'm basically a cash man, Gordon. It was the tradition in my family. We were Kulaks, you see. I'll have to think about it. Let's have a glass of the Macaskill –' and Viktor put a paw around Gordon's shoulders. 'That's worth a journey from Murmansk and a force 11 storm on the way.'

'The American,' said Gordon. 'He drank it like Coke. I'll not forgive him for that. A million dollars that will cost him. Oh Mac' – for he had spied him in the doorway – 'come and meet Viktor – Viktor Pinochkin. Viktor, this is Mac.'

Viktor was surprised at the appearance of the American. He had been expecting an executive, yet what appeared before him was more like a revolutionary. He had bare feet and was carrying his shoes by the laces. He was unshaven and his clothes were covered with wet sand. With his free hand he clutched to his chest a motley collection of pebbles and stones.

'Macintyre – Knox Oil and Gas Houston,' he said. 'I've got a card somewhere.'

'Pinochkin – Russian Fishing Fleet Murmansk. I carry my card with me everywhere.' Suspicious that he was the victim of some outlandish joke, Mac glanced at Gordon, who smiled blandly back at him.

'I'm here for the ceilidh,' said Viktor. 'We've been buying some fish in the Minch. You're doing some business too, I believe?'

Yes, but I'm not telling any damn Russians about it, thought Mac. He said: 'Could be.'

'Could be I like,' said Viktor grinning.

'Look, I think I'll just go upstairs and wash out these shells.' But Viktor was too intrigued by his little American to want to lose him so soon. 'What have you got there? A scallop, I think. When the two great powers meet we talk about shells, but not the exploding variety. That is good, da? So what have we here? Ah, the great scallop! See how it has unequal values – the right one, which you have here, is convex. The other flat. The two great powers with the third world vulnerable in between. Beautiful. The folds they radiate like the pleated dress of a dancer who pirouettes, and see how the grooves are, how is it said, striated. Just a shell, and yet so much to say of it. And here an otter shell, perfect like porcelain from China, and here like a thrush's egg, whose name I do not know – Gordon?'

'The pullet carpet shell – *Venerupis pullastra*,' said Gordon, scarcely bothering to look.

'Ah, but this little baby is our friend the razor shell. They call them spoots round here, Mr Macintyre. They taste so good, but how to catch them? They jet through the sand – strong little things.'

'I wouldn't want to eat them,' muttered Mac, who felt that truly the shells were no longer his but Viktor's and minded rather. However, he clutched them and took them off with him up the stairs.

Gordon called after him to come down for a drink when he was ready, and Macintyre said that he would. As soon as he had gone Gordon looked at the Russian and raised an eyebrow.

'But where is the Macaskill, Gordon? You are full of sheet, you know that . . .'

Passionately and with his toothbrush Mac worked away at cleaning the shells in his basin. Not until he had covered each groove and striation, each periostracum and tubercle and protoplax, did he feel easy in his mind again. He did not at first notice Danny watching him from the door.

'What you have there,' said Danny, 'is a bearded horse mussel – a nice example.'

'Yeh, yeh,' said Mac, piqued, 'and this is a scallop –'

'A *great* scallop, *Pecten maximus*, I would say.'

'And this is a razor shell.' Mac made as if to slice open his throat with it. Danny got the message.

'How's business? Need any help?'

Mac said: 'Urquhart's got all the powers of attorney. We should have a draft agreement by tonight.' He seemed depressed by the prospect and Danny showed no greater keenness when he asked:

'So we've swung it?'

'Looks like it.'

'No opposition at all?'

'They'll be doing all right. We're not robbing anybody.'

There was silence for a moment. Danny was thinking of the seals, Mac of the 'spoots' jetting through the sand. There was a moment when each might have said what he wanted to say, but the moment passed. There would not be another opportunity, and both suspected as much.

Danny said: 'Do they know what's going to happen to the place?'

'They're going to be rich. That's all they want to know.'

'Could I borrow the mussel, Mac, please? I have to show it to someone.'

'You'll bring it back?'

'First thing tomorrow.'

'OK.' Mac dried the shell on his shirt and handed it to Danny.

'Thanks. Good-bye.' It was not unlike a parting on a Siberian railway station. Mac did not want Danny to go and shouted after him: 'You speak Russian?'

'That's one of mine, yes.'

'You want the scallop too?'

'No, no, the mussel will do. Thanks all the same.'

'See you at the ceilidh then.'

'Right.' Danny left.

Mac collected up his shells and wrapped them in a towel, then turned on the cold tap to rinse away the sand remaining in the basin. The basin was brilliant white. Looking into it Macintyre was seized with vertigo. The drain was a black hole into which all creation would be sucked.

No it wasn't!

Danny Oldsen's fantasies had taken a seafaring turn and were awash with mermaids. But there was one detail which the story books refused (almost as though there were a conspiracy on the subjects) to elucidate. At what *precise* point did the mermaid stop being a fish and become a woman?

On the way to the ceilidh in the village hall he passed Gideon who, in what was left of the fading light, was repainting the name on the brow of his boat. 'Silver Dollar' was out apparently and 'Maid of Murmansk' was in. Danny watched for a while, then broached the subject of mermaids. Did they exist? Gideon had an appropriately Gaelic answer to this vital question.

'Well now, you wouldn't be asking me about them if they didn't, would you now?'

'Maybe not,' said Danny, working this out.

Gideon put down his paintbrush. The 'Maid of Murmansk' was not quite complete; as yet she was only the 'Maid of Murman'.

'There are two types of mermaid,' said Gideon, 'the home-breakers and the home-makers. There was one I heard of when I was a boy. She was washed up – let me see now – in Knock Bay. The Macleod boys found her on the beach one morning. She stayed with them for over forty years, married the younger one, though it was the older one who had lost his heart to her, and they had some family too.'

'She would be a home-maker?'

'I would say so.'

'And the other kind?' asked Danny. His romantic nature found it hard to accept the idea of a domesticated mermaid sending off for a special offer of tea-towels and tuning into Terry Wogan.

Gideon made a Gaelic gesture towards the sea and shook his venerable head. 'If one takes a liking to you, she won't be content until you're in there with her.'

'But what are they *like*?'

'Och, just as confusing as mortal women I would say – aye, well possibly more of a handful at the end of the day.'

'Are you being serious with me, Gideon?' The old man's answers had left Danny perturbed and dissatisfied. But Gideon looked at Danny straight and unblinking:

'I think so, yes,' he said.

9

THE CEILIDH

'Strange times, Archie, strange times'

From Scoone in the north to Crinan in the south the Ace Tones had acquired a reputation which other ceilidh bands could only wonder at. In the last year alone the Ace Tones had clocked up thirty thousand miles on their maroon Dormobile and had deposited more than twenty-seven pounds in the bank, a record to be proud of. Willie, who led the group from the piano keyboard, had dreams of a synthesizer, stacks of flashing electronic lights, and a regular date at a disco in Fort William, but was learning to be patient. Other considerations apart, Jock who played the fiddle and had been born A.B. (after the break-up of The Beatles) was too young to be allowed to play in hotels, for he lived with his uncle who was a minister of the kirk.

The ceilidh in the Ferness Village Hall was likely to be remembered for many decades, at least by those who remembered anything after a ceilidh. It was in the expectation of wealth beyond wealth that the villagers put on clean underwear, paid their three pounds to Mark on the door, and danced to the exuberant music of the Ace Tones. They were celebrating the

elimination of poverty in the western world; they were celebrating the possibility of dreams coming true.

Apart from Danny and Mac and Viktor Pinochkin, all the
celebrants came from Ferness, and everyone who lived in Ferness – all that is, who were weaned – had turned up for the
ceilidh.

Catriona had dyed her hair blue for the occasion, but had
kept the orange quiff which Rikki, who played the drums for
the Ace Tones, had been so rude about. Well, Rikki would pay
for that. Tonight she had decided to bestow her favours on
Danny Oldsen, who was both taller than Rikki and more important. Also he had a car. But then Catriona remembered that
she too would have a car just as soon as the money came in.
Maybe Danny would give her lessons in driving the thing. She
would have to be a better driver than Rikki. She grabbed Danny
and danced around with him. He was a bit stiff and reluctant,
but then this was probably his first ceilidh.

'Enjoy yourself!' she told him, and danced around with him
some more. Poor old Rikki! He looked like a shark with the
toothache.

Danny was hardly aware of the curiously coloured and coif-
fured creature who was thrusting him here and twisting him
there in approximate time to an old Tom Jones number. A few
weeks ago he would have been flattered by Catriona's attentions
and responsive to them, but now he was bewildered. What was
he doing here? This was never Marina's scene.

Mac, however blithely he had talked of 'the ceilidh', had not
at all known what to expect. *Playboy* had been mute on the
subject of ceilidhs. He had anticipated (and dreaded) something
with haggises and bagpipes in it, possibly even heavily bearded
clan-chieftains reading epic poems in the original Gaelic; but he
had reassured himself that, in this part of Scotland at any rate,
things rarely turned out as expected. As soon as he had paid his

three pounds (food included) he spotted Roddy serving behind a makeshift bar, and cheered up.

'Give me a forty-two-year-old whisky, Roddy.'

'Sorry, Mr Mac, we don't have any here tonight.'

'Well then, can you give me four eight-year-olds and a ten-year-old?'

Roddy could and did.

The Ace Tones were playing a Jimmy Shand selection and the rickety dance floor was crowded, so crowded that Danny was forced into uncomfortably close proximity with his punk princess. Viktor Pinochkin and Mrs Fraser, however, were clasped so tightly in each other's arms that it would have taken the Russian navy to separate them. Mr Fraser was not prepared to try. Seeing his wife blissfully embraced in the large Russian's bear-hug was excuse enough to get drunk, and, if she dared to accuse him of drunkenness the following morning, why then he would get himself the best divorce lawyer in Scotland. Did not the freehold of the general stores belong to him? And had he not negotiated a million pounds for it from Gordon?

For Gordon there was no holiday. He had grabbed Mac and insisted that while they were still sober they must complete all the outstanding clauses so that they could close the deal. But Mac seemed to have little interest in the matter. Two of the eight-year-old whiskies had gone the way of all whiskies, and a third was following them down.

'If,' said Gordon, 'we assess the useless land, the beach and the cliffs, at one third of the price of the working land and the village, we can justify the average price of two thousand per acre.'

'Sounds fine,' muttered Mac. How disreputable he looks, Gordon thought. Common courtesy might have impelled him to put on a tie.

'And then I'm asking for a tiny, tiny five per cent of revenue over ten years, that will be on top of the initial ten million, of course.' Mac made an effort to gather his wits and focus them on the tiresome business in hand.

'I can't say on the percentage, but you can have the ten million plus some form of reasonable participation to be mutually etcetera etcetera.'

'Five per cent,' said Gordon. 'Will *you* recommend it?'

'Oh sure,' said Mac. Sixteen years of whisky down, and twenty-six to go.

Ben had contrived a garment specially for such occasions as fêtes, sales, meetings of the Ferness Leisure and Athletic Club, and ceilidhs, anywhere where food was likely to be served. It was a heavy-duty combat jacket, and its lining contained numerous pockets. His beach-combing habits were so entrenched that he regarded anything on public display as belonging by rights to him. However, he would take no more than his stomach and his pockets could conveniently hold, and experienced caterers, such as Mrs Fraser who had catered this function, made generous allowance when baking the cakes or cutting the sandwiches or slicing the ham. So Ben, while Gordon and Mac were negotiating and the rest were dancing or gossiping, helped himself to a sponge cake here and there, a few scones, a pile of sandwiches and a half-dozen Penguin biscuits, nothing creamy or crumbly, nothing that would seriously be missed. The perishables went straight into his mouth.

Mark on the door had been working hard and had amassed a hatful of three poundses. When the crowds eased a little he was able to drink surreptitiously from the glass of whisky concealed beneath his chair. Although he was not old enough to drink spirits and was by nature a law-abiding lad, on this occasion he needed to get his courage up for there was something that had been troubling him excessively, that had been keeping him awake at nights, something that he could only discuss with the

Rev Murdo Macpherson. Murdo was late at the ceilidh. He had been practising his putting. From the base of the font to between the claws of the eagle supporting the lectern was a good twenty metres with an interesting borrow from left to right, but Murdo had improved his percentage until he could anticipate holing one in three. (Three in one, of course, was his target, although that would be miraculous.) By the time Murdo arrived Mark had emptied his glass and was ready to come out with what had been troubling him.

'There's a lot of uncovering of nakedness going on in the Old Testament, Reverend, mostly between pages ninety-eight and a hundred and forty. Have you noticed?'

Murdo had not noticed. It was some time since he had read the Bible, especially pages ninety-eight to a hundred and forty. But he praised the boy for bringing the matter to his attention and advised that he must try to see beyond the written word. 'If God talks about nakedness, Mark, then you can be assured that he has a very good reason for it.'

Mark considered this. It was not an aspect of the matter that had occurred to him. But what could the reason be?

'Mr Macpherson, Sir,' he asked in a shaky voice, 'have you got any Bibles with pictures?'

The moment had arrived for Viktor Pinochkin to sing his song. Viktor's song had come to mark a watershed – or a whiskyshed – at ceilidhs. Before he sang his song matters tended to be low-key, contained, cultural, polite and decorous; after he sang his song all hell might break loose. Was it the song itself which had such a liberating effect? Or was it Viktor's performance of it? We cannot tell. What is certain is that, once heard, Viktor's singing of Viktor's song could never be forgotten. Standing amidst the adolescent Ace Tones Viktor appeared a giant of a man. He had left his jacket with Mrs Fraser (she cradled her head on it ecstatically with the look in her eyes of a saint awaiting martyrdom) and his roll-neck woollen sweater turned him from a man to a grizzly bear. His voice – though not untuneful – was ursine too.

> 'Guess I was born to be a rover,' he sang,
> 'Guess I've always been a rolling stone,
> But some days when my rolling days are over
> I will find a place to call my own.'

Near the bar two old-timers were comparing notes; Archie from Cairn Farm and Sandy from Number Seventeen. Both were rather maudlin, drifting through the doldrums of drunkenness. Neither was alert enough to notice that Archie's wife had been as smitten as Mrs Fraser with Viktor and his virile way with a song.

Said Archie: 'Four generations of work on that farm, digging and draining and planting . . . years and years, and it comes to this.'

'Aye, strange times Archie. What was it now that Gordon offered you?'

'One and a half million in cash plus two per cent of the relocation fund and a share in the oilfield revenues . . .'

'Aye, strange times, strange times.'

Archie and Sandy considered how strange the times were, and then how rich they were both going to be, and then what a pleasant occasion a ceilidh really was when you took the rough with the smooth. Whereupon, since the attentions of Archie's wife were resolutely elsewhere, Archie and Sandy stood up and did a decorous jig to the second verse of Viktor's song, which was an approximation of the first but sung in Russian.

Having drunk about forty of the forty-two years of whisky he had paid for, Macintyre was losing his grip. Gordon would insist on completing his negotiations when he must have realized that this was neither the time nor the place. Mac's indifference spurred Gordon, who had cultivated a suspicious mind, to further efforts, for maybe this senseless capitulation on Mac's part was a particularly cunning gambit, the point of which would become apparent to Gordon *too late*.

'Come on, Mac,' he pleaded, 'we're still negotiating. What do you say?'

'What do I say what?' Mac giggled.

'Let's haggle. Dollars or pounds, the two thousand per acre and the ten millions? What about it?'

Mac giggled and shrugged and giggled again. 'Pounds. Let's say pounds.'

'You're meant to negotiate. Come on, how much have you got to play with, Mac? Mac, what's the game?'

'No game, Gordon, call it anything you want. Pounds, yen, rubles, cowrie shells, you name it.'

Gordon left the oilman giggling at a pile of cream cakes and made for the entrance to the village hall where there was trouble brewing. Willie of the Ace Tones was complaining to Mark and Murdo that the group was being underpaid. On Gordon's instructions Murdo had given them forty pounds. But, said Willie, they had got forty pounds at Christmas.

'What's wrong with forty pounds?' asked Gordon, arriving post-haste and relieved to find that there was still somewhere where his talents were appreciated.

'You only charged two pounds at the door at Christmas. Besides there's inflation.'

'We have inflation too, you know,' said Gordon severely.

Willie produced his clincher: 'Alan's got his new guitar now. You get the benefit of that.'

'He certainly plays louder.'

'Aye, well, that's good value too.'

Gordon felt beneficent. It takes great strength, he thought, to hold something very fragile and not to break it. It takes considerable maturity, he thought, to make concessions when one is not forced to. The effect of drinking on Gordon was to make him sententious. But he instructed Murdo to pay Willie the money out of the takings, and Willie to get the Ace Tones launched into a waltz.

'Give us a hand, Gordon, will ye?'

'If it's a slow one, Rikki won't like it when his girl's dancing with that lowlander and he's the drummer.'

'You're part of the rhythm section, and you'll just have to ensure that he falls in line.'

Gordon then pointed out that Murdo had given Willie five pounds short of the forty pounds agreed and Murdo paid up sheepishly. Gordon strapped on his accordion and followed Willie to the bandstand.

Mac was still staring earnestly at sponge cakes when Stella took him by the arm. She told him that they were playing a waltz. Mac remembered how Stella had danced with Gordon in the dining-room of the Macaskill Arms, and led her onto the dance floor.

Meanwhile Willie was reporting to the Ace Tones that he had finally screwed forty pounds out of that miser Urquhart (Gordon arrived just in time for that), and so they did not have to down bows. Instead they could play Moncrief's Lament which was in three-quarter time.

Said Rikki: 'If they get close, man, I'm not playing.'

'Listen, Rikki,' Willie said, 'if they could play while the Titanic went down . . .'

'Cat's not going down,' said Rikki with a suggestion of panic.

Wally was doing his Hollywood impersonations to Hamish, the only person in Ferness with the patience to indulge him. Wally's impressions were unique, for they were silent and involved no change of facial expression whatsoever.

He put his soft black hat on his head with the rim turned up and stared at Hamish challengingly.

'Who's that?'

'That's James Stewart,' Hamish guessed with some confidence, for it usually was. Wally looked at him contemptuously: 'That's Humphrey Bogart,' he said. 'No but watch ... watch *this*.' And he removed the hat.

'That would be James Stewart,' said Hamish happily.

Wally was rather offended. 'That's Clark Gable,' he said. '*This* is James Stewart.' And he put the hat back on.

Deep within the recesses of Hamish's brain something clicked. 'That's Humphrey Bogart,' he said.

'No, that's James Stewart.'

'To tell you the truth,' said Hamish, 'I'm not that much of a film-goer.'

Mac had enjoyed three moments of pure happiness since arriving in Ferness. One had been watching the meteor shower, one had been cleaning his shells; waltzing with Stella was the third. *Playboy* would not have approved of the waltz. *Playboy* might not approve of Stella – Mac could not imagine her naked on the centrefold with a cuddly toy under one arm and a staple across her navel. But Mac was beginning to doubt whether *Playboy*'s priorities were beyond criticism after all. He told Stella about his Porsche and about Lester's mechanical facility and about the place on Highway 16, and about the original Trudi. Stella merely repeated what she had already told him about his eyelashes.

But the waltz was as frustrating for Danny as it was fulfilling for Mac. Catriona seemed now to regard him as hers by rights, and Danny had eventually to be quite rude, to undo her fingers from his arm – she was a tenacious little thing – and to trot, even to run, to the exit. Catriona followed him, and sighed into the cool night air. The spider-shaped tattoo on her cheek looked like a large purple tear.

*

With everyone so enthralled in the glamour of the waltz Ben felt it would be ungrateful not to pay a second visit to the refreshment room. Mysteriously the pockets which he had filled to capacity just twenty minutes earlier now had plenty of room for further supplies. What could be the meaning of that?

After the last note of the waltz Mac and Stella held one another for a few seconds before breaking away.

'Oh gee . . .' Stella had whispered in his ear, but Mac had no idea what she meant. Mac glanced at the band, whose music had transformed his life, only to see Gordon standing at the front of the platform toasting him with a glass of something lethal.

Rikki had just sat down on the dais to finish his beer when Catriona came to join him. She looked, he thought bitterly, as though barbed wire wouldn't melt in her mouth.

'What did you want to go dancing with that prat for?' he muttered.

'What?'

'I saw you chasing that guy all over the dance floor, Cat. What's so special about him?'

'He's different,' Catriona maintained stoutly. Her multi-coloured hair stuck up all over her head. The spider was frozen in spatulate menace on her cheek, and her stumpy legs were encased in a sort of orange mesh.

'You're bloody right he's different,' said Rikki, who loved her after his fashion. She was delighted to see him jealous.

A few minutes later Mac could be observed sitting cross-legged on the ping-pong table. He had drunk all the whisky there was to drink and Stella had abandoned him. What was there to live for?

'Cheer up,' said Viktor, taking up a position on the opposite side of the net from Macintyre, 'it may never happen, and, if it does, you may find you enjoy it. You know that you have made everybody very happy.' Mac failed to respond. 'Prosit!' Mac lifted his empty glass and let it fall again. 'You don't believe that you are a success here? Then let me tell you something. You think this place is a kind of paradise on earth, am I right? Yet I am here to tell you that it is dying on its feet. It needed you just as it needs Captain Viktor Pinochkin to come and buy fish here and sing to the ladies. It needs your factory – you don't believe me? Yet people will get jobs. You can't buy scenery.'

Mac stared at the food, at the ping-pong table, at everyone except Viktor.

'It's their place, Mac. They have a right to make what they can of it, eh?' At last Mac managed a smile, so again Viktor said: 'Prosit! Cheers!'

'Yeh,' said Mac. It was the only remark he had addressed to the Russian since their first meeting.

'You speak a lot of sense for an oilman,' commented Viktor.

It was time for Mary's song. Mary was not from Ferness but from Gairloch, yet a ceilidh without Mary to sing one of her gay ballads and her brother to accompany her on the penny whistle would be more a barn dance than a ceilidh. The room fell quiet when Mary stood up to sing. Her face was pretty enough under its burnished harvest of hair, but there was a look in Mary's green eyes which suggested that she knew well of what she sang.

While Mary's brother played a plaintive introduction, Mary said she was to sing 'The Great Silkie of Sule Skerrie'. What, Mac wanted to know, was a silkie? Viktor explained that it was a seal.

'Danny said he saw some basking on the rocks.'

'I have seen too many,' said Viktor.

Mary sang:

> 'An earthly nourrice* sits and sings,
> And aye she sings, Ba, lily wean!

* *Nourrice*: nurse

Little ken I my bairn's father
Far less the land that he staps in.

Then one arose at her bed-fit
An' a grumly guest I'm sure he was:
"Here am I, thy bairn's father,
Although that I be not comelie.

I am a man upo' the lan',
An' I am a silkie in the sea;
And when I'm far and far frae lan'
My dwelling is in Sule Skerrie."'

Danny stood overlooking the jetty. There was a full moon and the sea sparkled like shattered glass. The poignant sweetness of the distant music and the rhythm of the waves comforted and consoled him. She would not come. Why should she come? But then she was there beside him.

'Hello,' she said.

She had not come out of the sea, for she was wearing a white dress which left her throat bare. Her skin was pale.

'Is everyone celebrating?'

'Almost everyone.'

'When do I get the good news?'

Oh dear. So she really had no idea. She thought it was all to do with her marine laboratory. Geddes had said that she was not a party to the scheme, but Danny had supposed she knew. After all everyone else did.

'I want to talk to you about that. There's a kind of alternative plan that's surfaced. Geddes knows all about it.'

'What do you mean?' Marina seemed more interested than concerned.

'What I mean is some kind of terminal here. An, um, oil thing.' But Marina received this information coolly, as cool as a fish. 'I don't see that happening here. I don't see that at all. That girl has a nice voice. It must be Mary Hamilton from Gairloch.'

> '"It was na weel," goo' the maiden fair,
> "It was na weel, indeed," goo' she,
> "That the Great Silkie of Sule Skerrie
> Suld hae come and aught a bairn to me."'

Somewhere over the bay the sky came alive. It was as though a huge curtain of multi-coloured ribbons had been released, or as though a cosmic dam had burst, and a rainbow waterfall surged through a sluice in the sky. There were reds and greens and blues shimmering and dancing. The air vibrated. The music of the penny whistle was plucked out on a myriad of united strings, a huge interplanetary accompaniment to Mary's tremulous voice.

'Holy mackerel!' cried Danny. 'What's happening?'

Marina glanced at the sky and smiled at it, as she might have smiled at a familiar friend in the street.

'It's just the Northern Lights – the Aurora Borealis. High energy protons and electrons spill over into our atmosphere; they get through our magnetic shield where it's weak, at the poles.'

'I don't care what causes it Marina, it's still beautiful. How often does this happen?'

'Any old time, although it's best when the sun's kicking up a magnetic storm. That gets the solar wind up and that's where the protons come from.'

'You say the darndest things, Marina.'

And still the universe trembled to the haunting song of the red-headed girl from Gairloch, as she completed the story:

> 'Now he has ta'en a purse of goud,
> And he has pat it upo' her knee,
> Sayin', "Gie to me my little young son,
> An' tak thee up thy mourrice-Gee.

"An' it sall pass on a simmer's day,
When the sin shines let on evera Stane,
That I will tak my little young son,
An' teach him for to swim his lane.*

"An' thu sall marry a proud gunner,
An' a proud gunner I'm sure he'll be,
An' the very first schot that ere he schoots
He'll schoot bath my young son and me."'

At the end of the song most of the villagers, adrift on a sea of
luxurious melancholy, left the hall, Macintyre and Gordon, still
with his accordion around his neck, amongst them. The Northern Lights awaited them.

'What the heck is *that*?' asked Mac astounded.

Gordon, as proud of the natural pyrotechnics as if they were
of his own manufacture, explained. Mac dashed back into the
hall, grabbed a handful of 10p pieces from Roddy at the bar,
and sprinted to the telephone-box. While dialling the intercontinental code and the Houston code and Happer's private
number, a complex undertaking after forty-two years of whisky,
Mac kept the door of the kiosk ajar with his foot, so as to be
sure that the lights didn't go out all over the sky.

It was the call Happer had been waiting for. He had had no
doubt that it would come. Macintyre's excited voice told him
what he needed to know.

'I'm watching the sky, Sir, and it's doing some amazing
things. It has everything, reds, greens, a kind of shimmering . . .
There's a noise too Mr Happer, like a faraway thunder, only
softer than that. I wish you could see it for yourself, I wish I
could describe it to you.'

'Be more specific, Macintyre. You're my eyes and my ears
there. Details are what I want to have, give me details.'

Mac stared out of the booth. Should he tell Happer about

* *his lane*: on his own

Urquhart who was leaning on a low wall and picking out the tune of the Great Silkie on his concertina? Should he tell Happer about Catriona who, having abandoned Rikki and having been abandoned by Danny, was looking like death and being hauled off to a fate worse than that by Mr Fraser? He made a desperate attempt to focus his befuddled eyes.

'I'll give you the colours first, Sir. Right now there's bright red – oh, no, that's the telephone-booth – white, green and blue, and it's like a heavy shower of all those colours.'

'Tell him,' shouted Gordon, 'that it's the Aurora Borealis.'

'I have some more information now, Sir,' said Mac feeding 10p's into the machine as fast as it could swallow them, 'it's the –' he took a deep breath '– Rorabora, and it's beautiful!'

'You're a lucky man, Macintyre. I haven't seen the Aurora Borealis since 1953 in Alaska, but I shall carry the memory with me always.'

'I haven't seen a comet yet, Sir, and I don't know if I'd spot one through all this Rorabora stuff, but this old guy said . . .'

Five thousand miles away in Houston, Happer left the telephone squawking aimlessly on his desk. Something more immediately urgent had caught his eye.

On the other side of the massive glass windows of Happer's office, suspended in a maintenance gondola like a large spider on a specimen slide, was Moritz. He was precariously engaged in sticking large letters onto the glass and smiling a sickly triumphant smile at Happer as he did so. The letters read:

'HAPPER IS A MOTHER F –'

and Moritz was about to add a U. While Mac's distorted voice continued to describe the 'Rorabora' Happer tried to claw at his tormentor through the double insulation hurricane-proof glass. Moritz mouthed obscenities at him, until Happer seized everything that came to hand, pencils, books, papers, everlasting flowers, an ash-tray commemorating the visit to Happer Tower of the Crown Prince of Roumania, an executive toy and a photograph of his nearest dependent female relative, and hurled them at the window. At length he had the sense to operate the automatic blinds, and Moritz vanished from sight, still smiling as the blackness shut him out, like an obsequious actor taking a curtain call.

Having used all his ten pences, Mac had been unable to complete his report to Happer, but Happer had already made a decision on the strength of what he had heard.

'Mrs Wyatt,' he said on the intercom, having gathered together as much as he could of the old authority, 'I'm leaving the office. I'm leaving Houston; in fact I'm leaving the country too. Would you have Crabbe look after things for a while, and I shall need the Leajet to take me to Washington to make the connection to Europe. I want a seat on Concorde to London with a shuttle to Aberdeen. Also, Mrs Wyatt, there's a maniac on the outside of this building. Call the police department to send some marksmen and shoot him off. Yes, and tell them they are to shoot to kill!'

As Egypt was after the Israelites quit it, so was Happer Tower after Felix Happer finally emerged. Crabbe, the heir apparent, could take no pleasure in his temporary and hollow promotion, Mrs Wyatt was overtaken within forty-eight hours by the menopause, and on Wall Street Happer stock fell by fifteen per cent (which dragged the index down twelve points). There was much speculation. Was he getting old, was he getting out, was he getting laid, was he getting married? But the rumour-mongers who picked at Happer soon enough found themselves with blunted beaks. The guy was gossip-proof.

And Moritz? They got him. What Mr Happer wanted, Mr Happer got.

Staggering back to the hotel under the Rorabora – curious how quickly even the most miraculous of natural phenomena loses its power to astonish – Mac, who was very drunk, decided to put a proposition to Gordon, who was rather drunk. When

Mac became very drunk he became sentimental. Walking along the sea-wall he had been sentimental about Ferness. Entering the bar he had been sentimental about the Macaskill, which Gordon was kind enough to produce. Having gulped a few drams of it, he became sentimental about Gordon.

'Oh Gordon,' he said and sighed. 'Oh Gordon . . .' He kicked the concertina, which protested noisily. Then he put his proposition to Gordon, asking him to consider it seriously, because, although he, Mac, might be a little tipsy, he did mean it, honestly and truly. Gordon agreed to consider it, and they both drank to that.

'Gordon, I want to swap with you – everything. I want to stay here and run the hotel and do some bits of business on the side and drive the cab and wear a silly apron like the one you wear. And Gordon, you can go back to Houston, take the Porsche – yeah, I mean it – the house, the job, the phone numbers . . . It's a good life there, Gordon. I pull out eighty thousand a year, plus I have over fifty thousand of mixed securities. I want you to have it all, and there's nothing due on the car – it's pure ownership. Oh, and Gordon, I won't let down your good name here, Gordon. I'll make a good Gordon, Gordon. What do you say, pal?'

Gordon raised his head from the glass, and looked around the small bar, smoke-stained and befugged, full of fake antiques and discarded dreams.

'What about Stella?' he asked.

'I was coming to that, Gordon. I love her very, very much – she's wonderful – she's the most beautiful woman I've ever loved and that includes Trudi and . . . heck, heaps of others. I think she knows it. I really think so. I want you to leave Stella here with me. Would you do that? Will you leave Stella here with me, Gordon?'

Very quietly Gordon replied: 'Sure, Mac.'

Macintyre shook his head vigorously to clear it of the whisky and everything else that clogged it.

'You're a good guy, Gordon.'

10

FERNESS

'A hatful of sand'

It was a quieter than usual morning in Ferness. The occasional
jet tore the sky apart and several bombs were dumped the far
side of the headland, but these had become domestic sounds
without which the inhabitants would have woken early,
alarmed, and looked out of their windows to see if the third
world war had started, for Murdo had been correct when he
had said that if the bombs fell here, they could not be falling
elsewhere.

The sky too was quieter than usual after the excesses of the
previous night. It was a hazy grey, pensive, inconclusive.

Mac and Viktor, having failed to get any breakfast in the
hotel, were sitting on a rock near the jetty, at ease in one
another's company.

'What kind of a car do you drive?' Mac wanted to know.

'I share a Volvo 145 Estate with my brother-in-law. A good
sturdy car – we've clocked up one hundred and twenty thousand and it's still the original gear box. Plenty of rust though.
The climate in Murmansk, you see, and the salt . . .'

'My car is a Porsche 930, turbo-charged. Here –' and Mac showed Viktor the photograph as a privilege of friendship. 'That's my apartment in the back, and if you look real hard you can see Trudi at the window.'

'What's the insurance like on a Porsche?'

'Very heavy, but I get a good deal through Knox Insurance.'

'You got a hi-fi in the car?'

'Quad . . . and video, but only stereo on the video.'

'I've got a quad outfit too – picked it up in Japan – where else?' Mac liked the Russian more and more. He took a printed card out of the wallet when he replaced the photograph.

'This is my address in Houston, Viktor, if you ever come to the States. Give me a call.'

'Ah, thank you so very much. Let me give you my address in Murmansk too, Mac. I'm not there a lot, but you never know.' Viktor handed Mac *his* card; embossed.

'How come you're here in Ferness?'

'Fishing. I've been coming here for years. I like it here, but it's a tough life for the locals. You should be proud of yourself, Mac, making them all millionaires.'

'I don't know,' said Mac, and truly he did not.

Gordon joined them, walking briskly from the village. Although he was not the sort of man to suffer a hangover he looked tense and ill at ease. Viktor asked whether breakfast was ready.

'We have a problem,' said Gordon. He sat down with them, but his shoulders were high and his back straight and he looked elsewhere than at them. Mac asked what the problem could be.

'The beach. Ben's beach.'

'What's the problem though?'

'Well, it really *is* Ben's beach. He owns the shoreline, four miles of it, from the grass down to the low-tide mark. I just found it in the Parish Records when I was checking out some title deeds.'

116

'Can he prove it?' the Russian asked.

'We can't steal the beach from him, Viktor. It's his.'

'You'll have to buy it from him.'

'It's not in the budget,' said Gordon. 'I thought the shore property covered the beach. I didn't make allowances for this.'

Gordon waited for Mac to take the bait. The telephone rang in the kiosk. A drunken villager staggering home from the neighbourhood of the village hall, where he had slept the night, answered the telephone as though he had been expecting it to ring. Through the glass the three men watched him in earnest conversation.

'Work out a price, Gordon,' said Mac with a tired hint of a sigh, 'and juggle the figures. Steal something from the Trust Fund capital . . . Something . . . anything.'

'Does he *know* he owns it?' Viktor asked, trying to be practical.

'I thought we could relocate him,' said Gordon. 'After all, it's just a shack, but this is different. Can't you stick in some more money Mac? It is a new property – at least it wasn't on the survey.'

Mac remained silent. From what he could remember of the ceilidh, he fancied that he had not been negotiating at full strength. He had made concessions that in normal circumstances he would not have made. He was essentially, he reassured himself, a Telex man.

The drunk emerged from the kiosk. 'There's a phone call from America, Mr Mac. A Mister Happer is coming to see you.'

Mac stared at him. 'Happer? You said *Happer*?'

'H – A – P – P – E – R – they spelt it for me.'

'Oh Jesus,' said Mac, as one communicator to another.

The American, the Russian and the Scotsman tramped across the sand towards Ben's shack, looking not unlike a trio of shady insurance salesmen. However, their mission was to buy and not to sell, and they would not have been able to get a foot in Ben's door because he had no door.

'Jesus,' said Mac again, because the strain was beginning to tell on him, 'how do you do business with someone who doesn't have a door?'

'The ethics are just the same,' said Viktor, but it was all very well for him. His career was not at stake. While Gordon tapped Ben's window-frame politely, Mac emphasized that he was prepared to release a further one million pounds for the beach, but not a penny more, and that that million must cover the cliffs and the rocks, even the big rocks; and the oyster-catchers.

'OK, OK, I get the message,' said Gordon, as Ben's grizzled head appeared through the window. He was wearing a flat tweed cap. 'Ben, can I have a word with you?'

'For sure,' said Ben.

Gordon introduced the others to Ben, and Ben to them. Mac was intrigued to find that Ben's surname was Knox.

'Can we come in, Ben, or will you come out?' Gordon asked.

'I'll just get the fire started,' said Ben and climbed over the sill. While he laid kindling on a heap of ashes outside where the door would have been had there been a door, Mac looked around him at the old boxes and planks, the driftwood and rusty iron that made up this old boy's demesne, and he had an image of Happer Tower like this. All it would take would be a small conflagration, two wires touching which ought not to have touched or a psychotic with a bomb in his coat pocket – a coat maybe like the coat Ben was wearing – and Happer Tower would be a heap of rubble in the sand. And out of it somebody would create a shack and lay a fire. Sand was the thing; that would always survive – even if the seas dried up, sand; even if the new ice age came, under the ice, sand, and – possibly – the Rorabora above.

'This is your beach, isn't it, Ben?' said Gordon.

'Yes,' said Ben with a hint of pride, 'it's been in the family for four hundred years. The Lord of the Isles gave it to an ancestor of mine. He helped him out with a spot of trouble, killed his brother for him – something like that.'

Viktor, not a man to tread delicately around a situation, but someone who regarded sledgehammers as the only nutcrackers, asked: 'You have a deed or anything? Papers?'

'It's in the museum in Edinburgh. It's a historical document.'

Gordon turned to Mac and invited him to make a contribution. But Mac had to overcome a certain coyness. He liked the old beachcomber and wanted to sit on the sand and share a pot of tea with him. He was a Telex man himself. But his duty was clear.

'Ben . . . what we wanted to ask you . . . have you ever thought about *moving*?'

Ben looked at him, as though he was being talked to in Japanese.

'No. No,' he said, and then, having considered the baffling question from all sides and found it still baffling, added more emphatically: 'No.'

This was as far as Mac could go without help. Gordon helped:

'Macintyre represents some people who think they have a use for the beach, Ben. They want to pay you for using it.'

'Money?'

'A lot of money,' said Gordon. 'One hundred thousand pounds.' Mac was shocked at the meanness of the cab-driving hotelier. The guy had a million to play with, and he started at a hundred thousand. He should work for Happer.

'You see the thing is,' said Ben with slow deliberation, 'I'm still working the place myself. It's my living. It supports me.'

'You would have lots of money, Ben. You wouldn't have to work.'

'Oh, we all have to work, Gordon,' said Ben. 'The beach has to be worked. Just think of the state the place would get into if I weren't around to work it.'

'Why don't we sit down around the fire?' said Viktor. In his experience nobody ever solved anything standing up. Ben collected various orange boxes and the one chair that was still intact and arranged them carefully around the burgeoning fire. Gordon resumed his pressure:

'It would help the whole community if Mac could use the beach, Ben.' Receiving no answer, Gordon glanced at Mac, then: 'Mac, how about if you made it *two* hundred thousand for Ben?'

'Sure,' said the Telex man. 'Two hundred thousand!'

'I'm sorry gentlemen, I can't. It's been in the family so long. I haven't the right. Would you care for your tea, gentlemen?'

'Oh yes, Ben, please,' said Gordon, and Mac and Viktor nodded. Ben hung the kettle over the fire, and smiled genially around his guests. There was no malice in the smile, no stubbornness, no triumph; it was merely a smile.

Danny had spent the morning scanning the sea from the window of his bedroom, but there were neither seals nor sails, neither mermaids nor merchantmen, nor Marina. He tried to recall all that he had said and what she had replied, and could not. He had worked hard to make her understand what was to happen to Ferness, the jetty half a mile long, the tanks that were to hold a million gallons of oil and more, and the refinery, so colossal that the whole of the village could have fitted within it and room to spare. At first Marina had laughed at his concern, but then she had looked at him quite seriously and said that no, it would not happen, indeed it could not for she had been promised the bay, and it was hers by right. All that he could recall, but later very little. Had they walked along the cliffs? Had he kissed her on the mouth and found it salty? Had he pointed to a crag to ask if she knew its name and turned back to find her gone? (The white dress like a falling leaf in the darkness

for the Northern Lights had long since burned themselves out,
and behind the hills the faintest violet hint of dawn.) But they
must have spoken of other things, of themselves alone, of themselves together. And had their mouths met just the once? How
had he got to bed? He had woken in bed, in his pyjamas, with
his suit neatly hung in the wardrobe, but the ceilidh had not
been a dream, and it was outside the village hall that he had
met her.

There was another mystery too. Viktor had joined their table
for lunch but he and Mac and Gordon, serving the food, had
been almost entirely silent, ordering the meal and taking the
order but nothing more. What had happened between them?

Now over the coffee Mac suddenly said to Gordon, who had
sat down at the table with them:

'Can this music be turned off?'

There were two levels of insult contained in this simple query.
It implied that Gordon (a) had poor taste in music, and (b) was
not master in his house.

Said Gordon: 'You mean you don't like it?'

'No.'

'You mean you *never* liked it?'

'No.'

'You mean not even when you first came here – you didn't
like it . . .?'

'No.'

'Yet you said nothing.'

'Nothing until now.'

'Amazing,' said Gordon, and remained seated.

As he, Viktor and Macintyre left the hotel to resume their
negotiations with Ben, Gordon untied his apron and handed
this, together with a dish-cloth, to Danny.

'Would you mind?' he said.

*

Ben thought Mac must be a lunatic, in which case Viktor and Gordon were presumably humouring him. When Ben saw Mac returning to his, Ben's, shack with the determined expression of an ageing scoutmaster on his face, he flinched. The afternoon would be wasted with all this talk as the morning had been, and the beach going to rack and ruin about them. But as laird of the sands hospitality was required of him, and he brought out from the recesses of the shack a bottle of Japanese brandy washed up in the April storm and two aluminium mugs. Mac had decided on a frank and straightforward approach this time, and had instructed Gordon and Viktor to leave him alone with Ben. The conqueror of Mexico, the rising star of the Happer Empire, should be able to do a deal with this old reprobate. But he no longer looked like a rising star of the Happer Empire. He was unshaven and wore an old cast-off sweater of Gordon's. His voice was plaintive.

'Half a million pounds is a lot of money, Ben, even enough to buy another beach with. Look, I have here a picture of a very fine beach in Hawaii –' He handed Ben a postcard which Trudi had sent him in the early days of their strangulated relationship. He had used it as a bookmark on the plane. 'Look at *that* sand, and those fine rollers, great for surfing Ben, and those palm trees. I'll buy you five or six miles of that beach, and you'd get the palm trees too or if you prefer The Virgin Islands or Australia . . . there are fine beaches there too.'

'It looks like a very nice beach, Mr Macintyre,' said Ben, glancing at the written side of the postcard, 'but I only need the one, and I've got the one, and I really don't need another, d'you see?'

Mac looked so dispirited that Ben stood up and patted him on the arm. He decided to offer the young man a more rational explanation, as well as more Japanese brandy.

'Besides, I don't know if there's a living in any of these beaches. You would have to go into that kind of thing in detail.'

'I'll buy you any beach you want Ben *and* I'll give you seven hundred and fifty pounds, which is more money than I shall ever see, to set yourself up with. It will give you some security in the early stages. Now what do you say?'

Ben decided to bring matters to a conclusion. The tide would soon be on the turn and he would have missed his opportunity of treasure-hunting for the day.

'You're great at talking with the big numbers, Mr Macintyre. You're good with numbers, are you not?'

'It's part of my job, yes.' Mac perked up.

'Well, how about this then . . .' Ben scooped up a fistful of sand from his beach and held it out to Mac, as though offering a sugar-lump to a horse. 'Will you give me a pound note for every grain of sand I hold in my hand? You can have the beach for that.'

Mac was suddenly alarmed, confused, awkward. How could he do a deal in sand-grains? How would they look on a company statement or audited accounts? He had no expertise where sand was concerned; he was a Telex man.

'Come on, Ben, we don't have to play games . . .'

'It's not a game,' Ben smiled and a trickle of sand ran out between his fingers.

'There, saved you a few pounds.'

Mac was tempted. He stared at Ben's hand in fascination. The sand danced before his eyes. But the thing went against all reason, all training, all that Knox Oil and Gas stood for in an ailing world. He turned his head away, and, almost sadly, said:

'I'm not here to play games Ben. We have to negotiate in a business-like way.'

Ben reversed his hand. The sand fell onto the beach. He shook his head slowly.

'Oh dear . . . oh dear. You could have had a very nice purchase there, Mr Macintyre. I can't hold much more than ten thousand grains of sand at a time. Did you think it would be a bigger number?' Ben's eyes were innocent and very blue. He looked directly at Mac without blinking.

'You took advantage of me, Ben.'

'Did I now?'

'How about a hatful of sand?'

'This hat?' Ben took off his flat cap and looked at it as though he had never seen it before. 'Oh no Mr Macintyre, that wouldn't be business-like.'

Watching from a near-by rock Viktor and Gordon could see that things were not going well.

'Ah, the Americans,' said Viktor, 'how did they become a world power?'

'Through Hollywood movies and Coca Cola,' said Gordon.

'Also the Ford car. But Ben is too gentle with him. He should remove his shoe and beat it on the table.'

'No,' said Gordon, 'Ben is not to be bought with money.'

'What does he love best? Every man has his price. This is not so, however, in my experience with every woman.'

'I think,' said Gordon, 'we should invite him to dine with us in the hotel.'

11

FERNESS

Happer's Comet

Gordon suggested to Danny that, if he wanted to make himself useful, which at the moment he self-evidently wasn't, he could serve the dinner. He, Gordon, would need to be with Ben and the others. Danny was agreeable and slipped quite naturally into the role, wearing his apron much as a Latin American general wears his medals, and serving the dishes with a theatrical flourish. He insisted on calling Gordon 'Senor', but Gordon chose not to make an issue of this, and the meal proceeded uneventfully.

It certainly was true that Ben enjoyed his food. He packed away such quantities of roast lamb, potatoes and sprouts that Stella had to send through what she had intended to keep back for Danny and herself. Nor was it merely the food that he enjoyed. It was years since he had experienced such obsequious attentions. To do so while remaining confident that he would never give in to them was doubly pleasant.

The atmosphere in the kitchen was tense. Many of the villagers were clustered there awaiting the news from the front lines, and others were in the yard outside. Moodily they picked at the remains of the roast meat until Stella slapped their wrists.

'You want to buy a house,' one inquired of the room at large, 'at half Gordon's price?' But nobody did.

Every time Danny appeared from the dining-room, the villagers looked up hopefully, but all Danny could tell them was:

'He wants some more sprouts.' Or: 'That's eleven potatoes he's eaten.'

These snippets of gossip were passed to the watchers outside who tried to put a favourable interpretation on them. But if their future prospects had depended on the number of potatoes Ben could eat they would have had no cause to worry; as it was, things looked bleak.

When Ben had eaten all there was to eat of goose pâté, meat and vegetables, trifle and cheese, and drunk a couple of bottles of a claret which Gordon had been keeping for Stella's birthday, he thanked them all politely and walked away whistling. The villagers parted to let him pass, but not without mumblings of discontent and muttered threats and curses.

Shortly afterwards Mac and Gordon emerged, walking rather fast to catch up with their quarry. When they did, Ben acknowledged their presence with his characteristic smile. Once Mac had been charmed by it; now he found it insufferably sly.

'You don't mind talking this thing through, do you Ben? I want you to see it from all points of view. There's no harm in talking, is there?'

'Of course not, Gordon.'

As they neared the beach they could see that the carmine-coloured sunset was being overlaid with vast bolsters of storm clouds from the West. But the sea was flat-calm.

'What if I told you that four hundred, five hundred people could make a living right here – if things were allowed to change?'

'Well, it wouldn't be the first time, would it?'

'What do you mean?'

'Local history, Gordon. This beach used to be a good living for three hundred people, imagine that. They gathered the seaweed and extracted the chemicals, ah, it was big business two hundred years ago. But then it became cheaper to get the chemicals from the Far East because the trade routes had been opened up, so the seaweed business went. The beach remained, but it was just a dump. Oh yes, that's when your people came, Gordon. When the arse fell out of the seaweed industry, and the landowners were driving the folk off the hills to make way for the sheep – there's a lot of things went on here, and I'm not talking about Bonny Prince Charlie and Flora Macdonald. If these people get the place it would be good-bye beach for ever, eh Gordon? For ever. And that would be that.'

They had reached Ben's shack. The evening was very quiet and rather sultry. Ben climbed through the window and re-appeared with some oranges.

'Have an orange, Gordon, Mac. I found this box on Tuesday on the rocks. I found a coconut once – God knows where that came from.'

While Ben stoked up the fire with the orange box, Mac asked him:

'What's the most amazing thing you've ever found?'

'Everything is amazing when you consider it, Mr Macintyre. And even more so when you ask yourself how it came to fetch up on this beach. I'll let you know the next time I get something *unusual*.'

And Ben wandered off to the back of the shack to empty his bladder.

'Should we get the priest to have a word with him?' Mac asked, but Gordon did not bother to answer. As he was about to peel his orange, he said:

'Shit! This is South African. I don't eat South African.'

Before Mac had time to wonder why Gordon should not eat a South African orange washed up on a Scottish beach, Gordon grabbed him by the arm.

'Look, there, by the Church . . .'

On the path below the Church it was just possible to make out in the fading light shapes and shadows of people, as though the dead had risen from their churchyard graves. They did not seem to be hurrying but they progressed steadily, quietly, and purposefully as the dead might.

'I was afraid of this,' said Gordon, as though to himself.

'Maybe they just want to talk to him.'

'There's an awful lot of them . . .'

The leading group had reached the glistening sand where the high tide had been. The orange sky was reflected in the beach, with between them the dark of the sea and the darker storm clouds. The villagers fanned out when they reached the beach, some of them taking the higher ground where the long machair grass grew, some on the very fringe of the surf; it appeared as if the entire population had come, but all in silence.

There was no leader, and they travelled in small groups of twos and threes and fours.

'Why did they come the long way round by the Church?' Gordon said. Mac huddled closer to the fire. He had seen films in which the hero defended himself from wolves by plucking a brand from the flames and thrusting it into the pack, but why should he need to defend himself from the villagers? He was their friend and wished them well. It was Ben they were after. But where was Ben?

Still they came. Mac could distinguish Roddy in his cowboy shirt and Catriona with her solid hair; there was Rikki without his motor-bike and Murdo with his arms high as though keeping the night away. Iain looked especially purposeful and Archie, who had stood to gain the greatest benefit from the deal, now appeared the grimmest of them all. Edward was there, and Mrs

Fraser with Victor – could Victor have been so treacherous? – and old Gideon carrying the baby Mac had wondered about that first morning on the jetty. Danny Mac could not see; he would be at the hotel with Stella – Mac felt a pang of jealousy – washing up the dinner no doubt. But no, there he was, running through the crowds, shouting out 'Marina! Marina!' and waving his arms about.

And then Mac noticed something else, something which he had been looking out for ever since he arrived in Ferness. A comet. Perhaps even Happer's Comet. Although he had told Happer he would know a comet when he saw one, Mac had worried that he might not. Yet here was – and he never doubted it – a comet.

It was a huge light in the sky, white, round and approaching fast. The villagers saw it too. First a group on the higher land saw it, then they drew the attention of those near them to it, and so on, a rustling like wind in the barley, until all had turned to face the sea, whence came the comet. They had reached a point, most of them, within a hundred yards of Ben's place, but were to advance no nearer. The light gradually approached the beach, and with it came a noise, which at first could only be distinguished by the younger among the villagers. A dog barked. But soon everyone could hear the noise and make out details of the comet. It had a tail (as respectable comets do) and on the tail rotating blades which matched the motor above the main bulk of the comet. Underneath it a steel structure, not unlike the giant runners of a toboggan. It was not, in short, a comet at all, but a helicopter, and it brought with it, besides the pilot, a very important man.

The chopper landed between Ben's shack and the crowds, and as the rotor blades slowed and became individually visible a large figure stepped out. Mac, Gordon and Danny moved forward to greet him.

'I'm travelling light, Macintyre,' said Happer, grabbing hold of Danny Oldsen's arm, 'just one bag in the luggage compartment.' He narrowed his eyes and peered through the gloaming at the walking dead. 'You didn't need to lay on this reception. This is by way of an informal visit.'

Happer began walking purposefully along the beach, keeping hold of Danny. Mac trotted hopefully on the other side of Happer.

'Since I'm here I thought we could organize a little presentation. Do these people need a church hall or a piano or anything? I'd like to make it a personal gift. The Happer Hall, that sort of thing. Let me know about it tomorrow.' Lowering his voice and turning to Danny, Happer added conspiratorially: 'And how about the sky Macintyre – anything new? We'll talk later, oh, and thanks for the call.'

'I'm not Macintyre,' Danny said. Had he waited any longer it would have been impossible to say it. Such was the power of the man's personality that he might have been forced to exchange identity with Macintyre rather than point out the mistake. But Happer did not thank him for it.

'Well, where the hell is he? I've been on the move for twenty-four hours. I don't want to play games.' He looked from the neatly suited figure of Danny to the tie-less unshaven Macintyre.

'Are you Macintyre?'

'Yes, Sir.'

Happer considered whether this was possible and decided that it was.

'Then get me a room.'

'Yes, Sir. This is Gordon Urquhart who has the hotel, Sir.' Mac added, somewhat curtly, to Danny: 'Bring the luggage.'

The two Houston men walked through the villagers who parted silently to let them pass. Gaining the higher ground they were no longer illuminated by the light from the helicopter, and Happer could pause to take his first lungful of Scottish air and to look at the sky. The storm clouds had receded and the sky was a dark olive green with a scattering of stars.

'Good sky you have here, Macintyre. Well done. There are one or two unfamiliar objects to look at up there, but I like this place. The air is good, clear. Get a telescope tomorrow, Macintyre – a two-inch refractor will do.'

Mac turned to Danny who was following with Happer's crocodile-skin suitcase.

'Hear that? I want a two-inch refractor for tomorrow.'

'Ben's got a telescope,' said Gordon. 'You'd have seen it if you'd been inside his shack. It's bigger than two inches though. It's about this long and this thick.' He carved out of the air something of the dimensions of a four-inch mortar.

'Jesus, Ben's got this whole place sewn up,' Mac muttered, but Happer was already almost at the hotel, and his young executive had to hurry to catch up with him.

The villagers were left alone on the beach with the helicopter, its pilot and Ben. It seemed there was not to be a lynching after all. But what did it all mean? Gideon was convinced that Happer was the President of the United States. He would have to repaint the name of his boat again in the morning.

Happer slept like a child in the big double bed which Stella shared with Gordon. It had been Stella's idea to move out. Multi-millionaires, she argued, need pampering. Whimsical creatures at the best of times there is no knowing what small courtesy may loosen their purse-strings.

'We will be moving back after Mr Happer has gone?' Gordon asked.

'He's a fine looking man,' said Stella. 'He reminds me of my father.'

At breakfast Happer was given pride of place, the big table in the window with Mac, who could have been a hired food taster in the employ of a Holy Roman Emperor – except that Happer insisted on cooking his own omelette and Mac had to make do with the kidneys turbigo which Stella had considered appropriate for a visiting multi-millionaire.

Mac did his best to brief Happer on the history of the negotiations, but Happer seemed confident that the business could be satisfactorily concluded.

'I'll offer *him* the piano, if he's the problem.'

'We've tried most things, Sir.'

'You try a piano?'

'No. We offered him beaches with palm trees and one and a half million dollars, but I don't know if he plays the piano.'

'And he owns the whole beach?'

'Yes, Sir. It's been in the Knox family for over four hundred years.'

'Knox, did you say?'

'Ben Knox.'

Happer stared stonily at Mac with a stare that seemed to hold him responsible for Ben having the name that had been grating inside his head for fifty years.

'I'm sorry, Sir. It's his name.'

Happer grunted: 'Since I'm here I'll talk to him. What's he like?'

Mac wondered how to describe Ben to Happer in a way which Happer would understand.

'Kind of eccentric, Sir, with an interest in local history. He roams the beach and he has an interest in the stars too.' This perked Happer up, so Mac continued: 'In fact he has a telescope – it's about *this* big.' Mac carved a telescope out of the air, exaggerating slightly Gordon's gesture of the previous evening.

'He knows the sky around here like the back of his hand.'

'Let's go talk to him,' said Happer.

As they strode across the dunes many eyes observed them. The smallest details were regarded as significant. Happer's giant stride was seen as a good sign; someone with such long legs was not someone to be frustrated in his designs. But man's capacity for believing what he wants to believe has always been enormous – especially where money is concerned. Mac kept throwing him useful bits of information, like a zoo-keeper throwing fish to a walrus:

'He has this trick he does with sand, Sir. If he offers you anything to do with sand say yes, we'll get him to sign something right away.'

'Sand?'

'Why, yes Sir. Anything up to about half a bucket full, say yes.'

Happer could make nothing of this. He had been alarmed by Macintyre's slovenly appearance. He liked his mind no better.

'He wants to sell me the sand?'

'No, Sir. You'll get the drift if he does the trick.'

'Don't worry Macintyre, I have a plan. I intend to offer him a telescope – a big one.' Happer's gesture indicated a telescope the size of an oil-tanker.

'Well good luck, Sir,' said Mac. But he was by no means certain that he wanted Happer to succeed. He went ahead of Happer as they neared the shack and called to Ben who emerged somewhat sleepily. When you live on a beach owned by your family for four centuries you do not always choose to rise with the herring-gulls. Happer's greeting was formal and patronizing. He was not used to meeting strangers and was out of practice.

'Delighted to meet you, Sir,' he said. Ben said nothing. He had been dreaming of wrecks and storms and foundering lifeboats and drowning sailors.

Mac said: 'Mr Happer has come from America like me.'

Happer offered his hand to Ben through the ever-open window. Ben shook it doubtfully and suggested that, if Happer had come that far, he had better come a few yards further, into

133

the shack. With some tactful assistance from Macintyre, Happer
climbed over the window-sill.

'That will be all for the time being, Macintyre,' he said.

All morning the helicopter sat on the beach. It could have
been a huge bird incubating its eggs. Some of the fishermen
inspected it gingerly. Anderson, the pilot, warned them against
touching anything red or yellow. They asked him questions.
Was there any place for bombs? Where did you buy them?
Would a helicopter come cheaper than one of those jets which
flew over Ferness?

'Sure would,' said Anderson in response to this last question.
'Those jets are fetching twenty million apiece nowadays. There's
big money in war.'

'More than in fish,' remarked one of the fishermen ruefully.

Gordon, Danny, Viktor and Mac waited on a cluster of rocks
a short distance from Ben's place, from the chimney of which
(made from the exhaust of a Sunbeam Talbot) a dribble of
smoke now rose. Laughter could occasionally be heard. The
morning passed. Mac took his shoes and socks off and picked at
some loose skin on his toes. Danny hummed the song sung at
the ceilidh by Mary Hamilton from Gairloch. Gordon, who hated
uncertainty as nature abhors a vacuum, strode up and down
and played the stock-market in his head.

A little after noon a face appeared at the window and Danny
ran to see what was required.

'They want some whisky,' he reported to the others; 'and
Ben wants some beef sandwiches with mustard and no salt.'

'Did Happer say anything?' asked Mac.

'He doesn't want any mustard at all. Just the salt.'

'Nothing else happened?'

Danny thought for a moment. 'I asked if they needed water
for the whisky, but –'

'OK, OK,' Mac muttered. He was familiar with this mood of Danny's, and was intensely irritated by it.

'Stay cool, Mac,' said Gordon. 'It's a good sign. I'll get the food.'

Viktor said: 'Bring some brandy back with you, Gordon. I'm dying.'

Half an hour later a formal procession could be observed crossing the beach. Gordon Urquhart led, carrying a tray on which was set the sandwiches and a bottle of the Macaskill. Then came Stella, upon whose tray was a jug of water, two tumblers, and a bottle of brandy which she threw to Viktor, who shouted: 'On the rocks!' and laughed heartily. Then came, out of curiosity, the fishermen who had grown bored of the helicopter, Roddy, and Edward pushing the baby, which was bawling as usual, but which stopped when it saw the Russian. Gordon and Stella passed the refreshments through the window of Ben's shack, then rejoined the others. Gordon produced paper cups and Viktor poured the brandy. The sun was hot and glinted off the helicopter. A fly buzzed. Somebody gave the baby some brandy.

'Slange everybody!' cried Mac, but the others merely looked puzzled.

'Skol!' said Danny, and everyone drank.

There was more laughter from the shack, then silence, then a burst of uproarious glee in which both voices joined.

To Mac the idea of Felix Happer laughing was altogether alien, but that he should be connecting with somebody like Ben Knox was unthinkable.

'Jesus!' he cried, 'What's going *on* in there?'

'Sounds like they're buddies,' said Viktor.

The sun grew hotter and the watchers sleepy. Archie, representing the villagers, crossed the beach to ask Gordon if there was any news about the money. Gordon said that there wasn't

– yet – and gave him a brandy. Viktor killed the fly that had been buzzing. Soon another fly started to buzz – or the first fly had been resurrected. Mac recalled his drunken conversation with Gordon after the ceilidh. Had Gordon meant what he said? Surely not. But yet . . . He glanced at Stella, whose eyes were full on him. She smiled, and raised her paper cup.

'Hey, it's quiet today,' said Mac. 'Where are all the planes?'

'Happer fixed that,' said Danny. 'The pilot told me. Happer didn't want to be disturbed, so he phoned London and told them it was a dangerous flying zone. Then . . . no bombers.'

Viktor poured himself another brandy. 'They'll be frightening somebody else's sheep today,' he said.

The sun went behind a cloud. A cormorant dived and re-emerged with a fish in its beak. The fish wriggled. The cormorant dropped it. Ripples spread. Nobody said anything. The drama had been self-explanatory. The sun emerged from behind the cloud.

'Hey look!' cried Danny.

Happer was climbing out of the window. Ben shook him by the hand.

'See you tonight,' said Happer.

He was a changed man. He stooped a little now and he walked more slowly, but he seemed younger and was no longer a man to be feared. Moritz would have been proud of him.

Happer strolled to the edge of the sea. Macintyre and Oldsen ran after him. Happer's nine hundred dollar suit was stained with sand and whisky, but he was smiling.

'Hello Macintyre.' He sounded welcoming and serene and there was something apologetic in the tone in which he addressed his subordinates, as though he were apologizing for not being the Happer Macintyre was used to.

'How did it go, Sir?'

'Fine, fine.' The billionaire seemed tentative, spoke slowly, as if straining to find the precise words to express what he had to say, as if alarmed at the decision he had taken. 'We have a lot of rethinking to do. There is a job to do here, but the refinery idea was a mistaken one. Ben has been filling me in. This place has a lot to offer, Macintyre. Ben has eight unplotted objects in this very sky right above us. We're going to start the scan tonight.'

He was going too fast for Macintyre.

'The acquisition is at a pretty advanced stage, Sir.'

Happer beamed at him, 'Oh I want the place, Macintyre – make no mistake about that. But tell Crabbe to re-think the refinery site when you see him tomorrow.'

Mac was confused. Had Happer said what he meant to say? Had he, Mac, heard him aright? But there was no time for elucidation, as Happer was well into his stride.

'I see a kind of institute here. A place of study and research. An observatory, so to speak, with radio and optical telescopes. Then, after a while, we could branch out.'

This was Danny's cue. If he waited, the opportunity might never recur.

'The sea, Sir! This is a natural place for a marine laboratory. We've already prepared some data at the Aberdeen lab; the North Atlantic Drift comes right in here, and it brings with it all kinds of things from all over the world. Ben will tell you.'

'Sea and sky . . . I like it. We can do good things here . . .'

Danny was learning fast. 'You could call it the Happer Institute, Sir.'

'Yes, you might be right. It might be just the name for it. The Happer Institute, that says it all. Good thinking. Write it down . . .' Happer tried to remember Danny's name. Danny supplied it.

'Oldsen, Sir.'

'You stay here with me, Oldsen. We've got a job to do. Macintyre, Crabbe is going to need you right away, so take the chopper to Aberdeen and get over to Houston. Tell Crabbe to start thinking along the lines of an offshore establishment, just for storage, and a refinery nearer the markets.'

'Tonight, Sir?'

'The sooner the better.' Happer looked more closely at Macintyre. Wasn't this the young man who had come into his office in that extraordinary tie? And to look at him now one could not believe that he was an employee of Knox Oil and Gas. Still, this was not a moment for scenes of a disciplinary nature. He contented himself with adding: 'And get yourself a shave, Macintyre.'

Happer was on his way back to the hotel when Mac turned to Danny:

'What's this sea laboratory thing, Danny? You didn't tell me about it.'

Danny seemed to have grown quite handsome in the glow of Happer's approval. The unshaven Mac was bitterly resentful of him.

'Och, it's just something I've been piecing together recently. Some of Geddes's people were working on it. Remember the girl?'

So that was it. Danny had been working surreptitiously through the girl. Well, good luck to him. She'd turn out to be another Trudi, no doubt, and where would that leave Danny if not in the lurch?

Happer was calling to him. 'You had better get moving, Macintyre. I'm glad I got here in time to stop the refinery caper.' He took Oldsen's arm and encouraged him away from Macintyre.

'Oldsen, get my overcoat and fix up some food for later. Ben and I will be full time on the telescope tonight.'

'Yes, Mr Happer.'

Happer looked at the sea which was full of crustaceans, and then at the sky, which would quite soon be full of stars, and then at Danny.

'Oldsen, I could grow to love this place.'

12

FERNESS AND HOUSTON

A pocketful of shells

There were suits in the wardrobe still in their plastic covers.
Mac's room in the Macaskill Arms scarcely looked as though it
had been inhabited at all. Mac packed them in his case, but
dressed in the one in which he had arrived in Ferness. Stella
had put a small bowl of wild flowers on the bedside table. There
was nothing he could do with them though. Maybe after he
had left they could go to Danny's room. Happer should have
had a large basket of fruit tied with a pink bow. After he had left
. . . Well, as a Telex man, he had done his best.

Gordon Urquhart was in the bar. As soon as he saw Mac he
handed him the bill on a small salver. There was constraint
between them. Now that he had to leave, Mac wished he could
do without all this. Press a button and be home in Houston.
Press a button and be in Houston.

'You don't really have to pay, Mac. I could stick it on the
Knox tab . . . anyway it's been fun having you.'

Mac had never seen Gordon so inept before, so clumsy with
words.

A POCKETFUL OF SHELLS

'No, I'll pay. I want to.'

'OK.' Slightly less gloomily he added: 'Make it out to Stella B. Urquhart. The B is for Beatrice. Her father was Italian. She's the boss.'

Mac wrote Stella B. Urquhart on the cheque and signed his full name at the bottom. That would be a surprise for Gordon.

'This is an American bank account, Gordon. It might not be valid here.'

'Don't worry. We'll stick it on the wall as a souvenir.'

'I hope things work out with Happer.'

'I think we can handle it.' But Gordon was not confident. Happer had said that he wanted the place, had spoken of observatories and laboratories, of an institute, but what did it all mean for Ferness?

'It's always the same,' he said bitterly, 'the big boys want the playground all to themselves.'

'At least,' said Mac, 'there'll be work around the place and money.'

'Yeh, work and money. It'll be OK.' But Gordon knew that the villagers would blame him. They could have done deals direct with Mac at the start, a few thousand, cash on the dotted line, better, they would argue, than this; far better. Mac held out his hand.

'Well . . . so long.'

'You should say good-bye to Stella. She's upstairs.'

Mac remembered what had been said after the ceilidh; Gordon did too, for sure. The whiskies, and that haunting song, and the sky ablaze with coloured lights . . .

'No,' he said, 'it really doesn't matter.'

'Go and see her, Mac,' Gordon said. His voice was quiet, but insistent. Let him insist all he liked, Mac was not going upstairs.

'You say toodle-loo for me, Gordon. And toodle-loo to you too.'

'Have a dram of the Macaskill. Then I'll see you off.'

*

Danny had been waiting on the rocks, scanning the sea. He had such important news for her, she would surely come. And how pleased she would be! Geddes and Watt would have to be involved too, but it would be *her* project. She was the oceanographer.

But it was his doing. Happer had been talking about the sky, but he, Danny, had reminded him of the sea; if it had not been for him . . . He wanted to tell Marina about it so much.

He had been staring at the sea for such a long time that, when she finally appeared, just her head in the face-mask above the grey waves, he was not certain that it was really her. It could have been a piece of driftwood, or a rock exposed by the receding tide, or a seal. But then the more he stared the more certain he became that it must be her, and so he shouted out her name several times over. Did she wave? Of course it was not easy to hear much wearing one of those things, so he shouted again and again. He told her about Happer, and the laboratory, and how he had made it come about, and then, to make certain she understood, he waded into the water after her, in his smart clothes and Italian leather shoes, just as he was, first wading and then swimming. The waves were quite high this morning, and the current was running fast, so that he had some difficulty spotting her once he was swimming. The light played tricks, but he was sure he would find her all right if he kept shouting her name, which he did. She would be so pleased . . . so pleased . . .

The chopper blades were already turning, as Anderson helped Mac into the passenger seat, explained to him about his safety harness, and handed him his headpiece to protect his ear-drums from the noise.

'It'll not take long to Aberdeen,' he shouted. Gordon, Stella and Viktor were there, watching from a distance. Viktor was waving. A few of the villagers had turned out, but after all it was the middle of the morning on a working day. Happer and

Ben must have been working, for they were still together in Ben's shack, where they had spent the night. There was a lot of sky to chart and Happer was thrilled to find it dotted with surprises.

As Anderson revved up the engine, there was a tapping at Macintyre's window. Anderson showed him how to open it, and there was Iain, who had been so keen to help him make his first telephone call to Houston.

'Excuse me, Mr Mac, can I get your autograph please?'

As the helicopter gained height Mac was able to see that the water, which appeared so formidable from the shore, was placid and translucent from above. He could see how the shelves of rocks gradually gave way to deeper water, and how shoals of fishes appeared as shadows. He thought he could see somebody swimming a hundred yards or so from the shore – there was certainly a disturbance of some kind – but possibly it was no more than waves breaking over a rock.

From the shore, from the dunes, and from the village, the inhabitants of Ferness shaded their eyes to watch it go.

'Is that the yank in the aircraft?' said one.

'That's him OK,' said another.

'Bugger it,' said a third, 'he never said cheerio.'

Gideon, the prow of his boat blank as he awaited inspiration for a new name, saw the helicopter pass, and decided to call it 'The High Flier'. Stella watched it go, and had thoughts concerning Mac's departure which were so weird that it would be improper to detail them here.

The Reverend Murdo Macpherson, preparing to drive off on the seventh hole, a tricky dog-leg to the left with plenty of sand to catch the unwary, missed the ball entirely and pretended to himself that he had only been preparing to drive. He preferred to play alone, watched only by God.

From the helicopter Ferness appeared like a model village, so small and self-contained that one could almost lift it out of its hole in the sands and give it to children to play with.

The colours of the houses and the beach were like toy town colours; the helicopter moved into cloud, and for a moment the village was framed with a border of white, like an old Christmas card.

Anderson spoke into his radio:

'Aberdeen approach . . . This is Golf Yankee Yankee at flight level four five estimating the zone at three zero.'

And Aberdeen control replied: 'Roger Yankee Yankee. Listen out on Scottish one two four decimal nine. Call approach on entering the zone. Out.'

Mac's penthouse apartment seemed barren of charm. The Louis Quinze style mirror and the reproduction Azerbaijan carpet tinselly and cheap. There was a pile of letters on the mat, but none of them written by real people in handwriting except, that is, a note from Lester about the Porsche. It was in excellent order except for a dent in the front nearside wing which must have been done by some hit-and-run freak. He switched on the air conditioning; its familiar hum almost deafened him. He moved through to the kitchen and checked the freezer. It was bare except for an unidentifiable piece of cheese, which was almost all rind, and a bottle of Seven Up.

From the pockets of his light-weight raincoat he removed his shells, the mussel, the scallop, the other shell, the pullet carpet shell and the razor clam, and placed them carefully on a blue-tiled working surface. They looked very important. Mac picked up the razor shell and held it to his nose. Faintly, very faintly, he could smell Ferness.

Also from his pockets he removed postcards of the place and a few Polaroid photographs – Gordon, Danny and Viktor, the beach with the telephone-booth in the foreground, and Stella laughing – which he pinned up on his workboard, next to his year-chart and memory-jogger. Then his memory having been jogged, he dialled a familiar number on the phone, and, while waiting for an answer – it seemed as though there might not be one – opened the glass doors which gave access to the balcony.

There was Houston, and Happer Tower, and, in the distance, Highway 16. White lights approaching, red lights retreating. The city was alive with lights – so many and so bright that, when Macintyre looked into the sky, no stars were visible.

Inside the apartment the telephone was answered – Trudi's flat-mate or answering service. As Mac picked up the phone he glanced at the shells, and at the photographs on the workboard. The shells were chipped. The photographs would not last long before they began to fade in the harsh Texas light.